BULLET BOOKS
SPEED READS

ON A PLANE . . . ON A TRAIN . . . FASTER THAN A SPEEDING BULLET!

MAN IN THE CLIENT CHAIR

BULLET BOOKS
SPEED READS

#6

Manning Wolfe
Jay Brandon

STARPATH BOOKS, LLC

AVAILABLE NOW

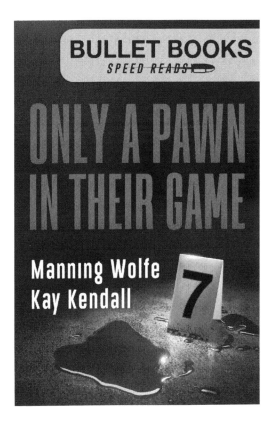

SPY GAMES . . .

Sammy expects a carefree summer during her internship at the US Embassy in Vienna. Competing spy rings clash in desperation and threaten her life as every Strauss waltz accompanies a murder. Is the handsome stranger she meets heading for romance or using her as a pawn?

Can she figure out who's playing the tune before the dangerous dance ends badly?

MAN IN THE CLIENT CHAIR

Chapter One

When Steve Lewis walked the prospective client into his law office, he thought the man was going to take the padded, high-backed chair behind the desk. The glare he gave the client chairs said clearly they weren't good enough for him.

Then the client shrugged, as if to say he wouldn't be here long, tossed his expensive jacket across one chair and sat in the other, arranging himself to fit. There was plenty to arrange. He was a big man, tall and hefty, the kind of added weight that makes a man look imposing, not soft. He stared at the lawyer until Steve sat down behind the desk. The man hadn't offered his name or his hand.

The man had a strong face, a good stare. Aquiline nose, broad forehead, under a full head of almost-too-long, graying brown hair. Body verging on stout, but with the stature to hold that at bay a few more years. He waited, giving Steve a chance to form impressions of him, which Steve did. More than the man would have guessed.

1

The visitor only glanced at Steve, taking in his appearance including his blue eyes, brown hair, and broad shoulders that usually drew longer looks from women. The client scanned the credentials framed and mounted on the wall behind Steve's desk—diploma from Yale Law School, Order of the Coif, a picture with a legislator at what appeared to be a fundraiser. The legislator wasn't particularly prominent, so it must have been a personal connection. The visitor seemed satisfied, if only barely.

He looked directly at Steve and said, "My wife is missing."

Before Steve could express his condolences, the man continued. "I'm glad. If she's just run off, good. I can't stand being married to Joanne anymore, and she hasn't given a damn about me in years. But if she's dead, especially if she's been murdered, I need to know. Because, of course, I'd be suspect number one. Maybe one of my enemies is counting on that. Maybe one of them lured her away. Maybe they killed Joanne just to set me up for it." He paused before adding, "This is a privileged conversation, isn't it?"

You'd better hope so, Steve thought.

"Of course, unless you tell me you're planning to commit a crime. Don't do that, please. I'm a lawyer, not a detective. I don't find missing persons. Why have you come to me?"

"I got your name from a colleague. He said you handled his daughter's property settlement, very favorably for her. I want you to file my divorce for me, with as much publicity as you can manage. That should draw my wife out of hiding, if that's what she's doing."

"Why don't you just go to the police, tell them she's missing? It's been more than twenty-four hours, hasn't it? They'll open it as a missing persons case. They're better at turning up people than the press are. Let the professionals do their job."

The man looked at Steve as if realizing he wasn't bright enough to hire. "Because A, I actually do want a divorce, and B, going to the police would involve them questioning why she might have left, or in fact what might have happened to her. That's not how I want to present this to the public. I want to say she left me. And, I'm not sure I agree with you about the police being better than the press."

"Ah." Steve understood. The client didn't want the police looking into his affairs, so to speak. "This way you can guide the story the way you want."

"Thank you." Now the client—prospective client, actually, as Steve was far from sure he wanted to take him on—had decided that this lawyer was smart enough to hire after all. For just a moment, as the man stared at him, Steve had seen him thinking, *Now I have to kill you*, because he'd already told the lawyer too much.

"The police will start looking into it anyway, you know," Steve said.

"I do, but this way they start with the perspective that I'm the betrayed husband. And I'll be able to tell them this isn't the first time she's run away with a lover."

It's not? Steve thought. Interesting phrasing there. *I'll be able to tell them . . .* He refrained from asking, because it would make the man in his client chair question his intelligence again. Whatever his wife had done in the past, the client could tell the story, tell what his wife had done to him. He could say he'd kept quiet about her behavior for years, but just couldn't do it anymore. Steve could see the press conference already.

"I'd like to speak to some of the people who know you both, work up some background information, get some perspective on your history," Steve said.

"No problem. You can speak with our housekeeper of thirty years, Barbara Stands, and either or both of our children."

"That should do."

"My assistant, Trevor Prentice, will contact you with the details. You may speak to him as well."

Steve nodded knowingly. The client stared back at him with what Steve took for approval. The man took a check from his shirt pocket, filled it out, and handed it to Steve. "Will this cover your retainer?"

Steve didn't look at it. "Yes."

The man gave Steve a very quiet, knowing smile, having just bought the lawyer, or so he imagined, and stood up to leave. He stopped at the doorway, turned back to Steve, and said, "You do know why you won't have any trouble generating publicity once you file, correct?"

"Yes, Senator. I know."

Chapter Two

Steve heard the client go down the hall back toward the reception area and exit. Steve wondered about the scene in the outer office in the few seconds before he heard the main door closing. Did the senator bother to flirt with Loni, or just assume she, too, was his for the asking whenever he felt like it, as powerful men were known to think? He'd be very, very wrong about that.

Loni came in for the report. She stood across the desk from him, not even glancing at the client chair. Nor did she bother to ask a question, except with a raised eyebrow.

Loni was a medium-height brunette, though she could, Steve would swear, change either of those features at will. Sometimes she could look him levelly in the eye, sometimes when she put her head against his shoulder he would swear he could slip her into his pocket. She was slender but strong, and it seemed she could also shift the contours of her body whenever she desired. Or maybe it was the weight of his stare that did that.

"How was he with you?" Steve asked, finding he was still curious about the way the senator had treated her.

"He tried to charm me. He thought he did." She shuddered.

"Think he could be a killer?"

She'd watched and listened to their entire conversation on the closed circuit TV, of course. She stared at him, then finally shook her head slowly. "Ordering it, maybe. Hiring it done. Doing it himself? I don't think so. He seems paper thin, all facade."

Steve nodded. He thought so too. But, he also thought first impressions could be wrong. "Did you believe him?"

"Partly," she said.

"Which part?

"The part about it being hot outside. I just came back from lunch."

"You are so hard."

She gave him a look, then said, "I take everybody at face value, once the check clears."

"You at least know that was Senator Winston, don't you?"

"I know he looked very much like pictures I've seen that purported to depict the alleged senator."

"I repeat . . ."

"Yeah, yeah. Right back at you. Seriously, Steve, you know this stinks, right?"

"Which? His story, the setup, what I'm supposed to do?"

"Uh-huh."

"Since Maryland is a separate property state, what's his is his and what's hers is hers, do you think this is about old-fashioned greed instead of adultery?" Steve asked.

"I think it's about everything in a bad marriage," Loni said.

"So what? You think I should tell him thanks but no?" Steve asked.

She looked thoughtfully at the check she'd picked up from his desk. The figure impressed even Loni. "I think we should do what he's paying us to do. For now. Maybe we interview the house-keeper and his aide and decide whether to take him on after that," Loni said.

"We don't have to cash the check yet," Steve said.

She turned and walked out, with a little extra sway because she knew he was watching.

Loni was actually licensed to practice law. Some days she liked it more than others. A couple of times, they'd done a setup where she was the lawyer and he was the secretary, very for-ward-looking and chi-chi. Sometimes, they just presented them-selves as co-practitioners, but they knew a traditionalist like the senator would want to see a pretty woman behind the front desk and a man behind the inner one. So that's how they'd played it this time. Regardless, when a client hired the firm, they both worked on the case.

Darla was their secretary, paralegal, and jack-of-all-trades, but they sent her on errands when a client of a particular type came in. The fewer who knew the identity of their roster, the better. They'd bring her in on the file once things settled. Or not.

Besides, Darla didn't have Loni's long legs and charming smile. The attributes that had attracted Steve the first time they'd met. One could get a good tale from Steve about how he and Loni got together. It was a story in progress.

Chapter Three

Steve had met Loni when he was in his last year of law school at Yale. She was a 2L, a year behind him. They were both on the mock trial team and were on opposite sides of a case involving corporate fraud. He was lead on his team, and Loni was assigned the role of arguing the company being acquired had knowingly overvalued its assets. In other words, they were opposing each other, the first time they ever met. Steve laid out the facts of the case for the mock jurors, showing the CFO of the acquired company had sent an email to the CEO saying the company had an asset, a subsidiary, that had recently dipped in value.

Loni tripped him up when she showed it was impossible to prove that the email had ever actually been sent or received and besides, she threw in for good measure, the CFO hadn't been involved in the negotiations.

Breaking the rules of the competition, Steve exasperatedly asked her directly, "How could the chief financial officer of a company not be involved in a merger negotiation?" Without a beat Loni replied, "Because she's a woman and no one values her opinion." Looking up at the mock trial judge, Professor Martha Hughes, and seeing her expression, Steve knew he was screwed.

But by one of the best. He admired anyone who could beat him at his own best game. Before the smoke of the debate had dissipated, he asked Loni out for a beer and the rest was history. They were never apart for more than a day after that.

Steve clerked for a federal judge in Connecticut while Loni finished her third year at Yale. Neither wanted to work for big law, although both were sought after by firms in New York, Chicago, and Dallas. After Loni finished at Yale, Steve asked her to marry him. The judge Steve had clerked for presided over their wedding ceremony.

When it came time to decide where they would establish their practice, Steve prioritized his love of sailing and they chose Baltimore. The two hung out a shingle and started putting the word out that family law was going to be their specialty. It seemed to offer the most interesting story, and Loni said she would prefer to help a man or woman through the most difficult time of his or her life rather than hold a corporation's hand during a painful merger. A year later, they were both board-certified in family law, which put them on a list with the State Bar of Maryland as having expertise in divorce, adoptions, domestic violence, and guardianship. Their practice grew quickly, they kept their overhead low, and they never had trouble paying the help or the electric bill after the first year.

When a local teenager wanted to divorce his parents due to abuse and neglect, Steve and Loni filed the petition. The mother had killed the teenager's sister during a heated fight over a dress belonging to the mother, and the young man was forced to stay with his father. Steve and Loni proved the father was still emotionally involved with the mother to the detriment of their son, won the case, and made a name for themselves. That case stepped them up to higher-end clientele and they bought a nice house. They coasted on that for a while, and Steve invested with two other attorney sailors in a Jeanneau Sun Odyssey 440, a large single-hull sailboat that they kept at the Baltimore Marina.

Now, they had another high-profile case but on a national scale. The senator was surrounded by scandal and intrigue. They couldn't create a better setup if they'd scripted it. On the other hand, the pitfalls were obvious, starting with whether they believed anything about their client, including his story, his background, his wife's infidelity. Loni even questioned his hair.

Chapter Four

Steve and Loni met the Winston housekeeper on a typical Wednesday afternoon in a home that was far from typical in stature and décor. The foyer was over three stories high, with a winding staircase peeling off to the right. The wrought iron railing was designed to impress, and the inlaid Italian marble stairs were only used for making a grand entrance at the occasional fundraiser or Christmas charity event.

Loni guessed there was an elevator hidden somewhere for the vertically challenged and various deliveries. Barbara Stands was a woman a little past middle age who kept herself in good shape, possibly by jumping every time she heard her employer speak. Her British accent suggested she'd not bothered to acclimate to American English, and her soft hands suggested she'd not done housekeeping in a long while. She seemed very efficient. The hands, while soft, looked strong. Her posture was brilliant. She had very pleasant features and medium brown hair in which she didn't attempt to hide the gray.

"I manage the staff here in the house, the grounds, and gardens," Ms. Stands said. "I was the governess for the children when they were young, but both little darlings have graduated from college and moved into their adult lives."

"We haven't met with them yet." Loni sized her up. *Little darlings?*

"We'd like to get a picture of the Winstons' home life," Steve said.

"Such as?" Ms. Stands bristled and grew an inch when she straightened her posture. She was a formidable woman.

"We would normally modify our questions with manners, but this is a divorce and we need to know the details that could come out if there's a court battle," Loni said.

"Court battle? I've never seen the Winstons say a cross word to one another."

Well, there was the first lie, Loni thought, and it would probably set the tone for the rest of this interview. No one gets to a divorce without friction, and any housekeeper worth her salt would know what's going on in her place of work, especially one with an attitude like this one.

The housekeeper didn't seem to have chosen a side in this battle, at least not obviously so. Maybe they could use that to their advantage.

"When did their marriage start to deteriorate?" Steve asked.

"If you must know, the trouble began when Mrs. Winston's friend, Sally Salinas, was murdered. Actually about a month before."

"Murdered?" Loni asked.

"It was in all the papers and on the TV news. I hope the same fate has not befallen Mrs. Winston. I'm worried sick about her disappearance." The stately housekeeper actually wrung her hands. Loni had heard that expression her whole life, but didn't think she'd seen anyone actually perform it before. It fascinated her, like finding a guide to manners from a previous century that advised young women never to be the first to speak.

"Is it common for her to disappear?" Steve asked. While Loni studied the housekeeper like an *objet d'art*, Steven continued questioning her like a cop, routine. It made people feel obligated to keep responding.

"Yes, but not this long. She's gone off to spas or to shop in New York, but she always checks in within a day or two." Ms. Stands seemed truly distressed.

"Who murdered her friend, Sally Salinas, and when?" Loni asked.

"It was about three years ago. Her murder was never solved."

"How did that manifest as trouble in the Winston marriage?" Steve asked.

"Senator Winston advised that I should not allow Sally Salinas in the house if he was at home. Mrs. Winston entertained her in the solarium or the gardens when the senator was at work, but the two women always finished their conversations before he returned home in the evening."

"Why did he ban her from the house?" Steve asked.

"I don't know, and I didn't ask him. Mrs. Winston said the senator thought Sally was a bad influence on her. Something about gossip and stirring up trouble."

Trouble, right here in River City, Loni thought.

Next stop was the Capitol Bar and Grille for a meeting with Trevor Prentice, the senator's aide and purported confident.

Trevor was tall but slight, very well dressed in a three-piece lightweight gray suit. He looked completely at home in the Capitol Bar, a well-known watering spot for the more prominent rhinos and elephants of Washington politics. The walls were adorned with paintings of English-looking landscapes and, in the hallway leading to the restrooms, caricatures of local celebrities, meaning politicians. The décor was old-colonial men's club updated, featuring tall tables with high stools so people would be just as tall sitting as standing. In fact, one only had to lean back on the stool a little to be some combination of both.

Trevor looked Steve up and down in a way that annoyed Loni, but then Trevor turned his attention to her. Trevor was blond in a way that made Loni suspicious, but his blue eyes were completely authentic, framed by long lashes.

"I'm quite sure I can't help," he said quickly. "I don't get involved in the senator's personal life."

"But you must know his wife well," Steve said. "You couldn't do your job otherwise."

Trevor appeared properly stroked. "Of course one needs to know certain things about the domestic arrangements. I'm just saying I didn't pry."

"Of course not," Loni said. "The senator would quite naturally confide in you. Isn't that part of your job as his confidential aide?"

Trevor smiled. Steve was pretty sure Loni had just given him a promotion, and Trevor obviously appreciated it.

"Yes, it is; thank you. People think you're a snoop if you're doing everything you can to make your boss's life easier."

"Very few people understand the dynamics of working closely with someone in power," Loni said.

16

Steve gave her a *who are you?* look that she ignored.

"Exactly," the aide said, leaning forward and lightly touching her knee with one fingertip. It didn't seem flirtatious, more like she'd gotten him and very few people did.

"If you're trying to suggest the senator had anything to do with his wife's disappearance, or is somehow setting her up, trust me, you do not know the dynamics of their marriage," the aide said, crossing his legs on the high stool.

"Of course we don't," Loni said. "We've never laid eyes on Mrs. Winston. So enlighten me."

Steve and Loni could both tell when an interviewee was connecting better with one of them than the other. This was definitely one of those times. Steve pretended to get a call on his silenced cell phone, made an *I have to take this* hand gesture, and withdrew to a far wall. He invented a fascinating imaginary conversation while his eyes went everywhere around the bar.

Trevor also looked around the bar, eyes going left then right. Loni was tempted to emulate him, but figured he'd cased the joint well enough for the both of them. Leaning in closer, Trevor said, "The senator had no need to screw over his wife. She'd already . . ." He trailed off and leaned back, looking as smug as a cat with a secret.

"Screwed herself?" Loni guessed. "Or rather was being screwed by someone else?"

"Those are your words, not mine," Trevor said primly.

"Well, I didn't invent them. They're only mine because you wouldn't say them. But that's where you were leading, right?" She gave him a very specific look, one of dawning admiration for someone of obviously superior intelligence and vast knowledge.

17

There was a rumor some man somewhere had been able to resist this look, but the rumor had never been verified.

Besides, Trevor was a low-level Washington insider. Gossip was his oxygen. "Yes, that's what we all heard. Not about anyone specific, just that she was seen slipping away from her normal schedule, let's say." He looked around again. "She was a woman with time on her hands and still a young woman at that."

"Hmm. So Senator Winston doesn't really care, he just . . ."

"No, I think they both stopped caring in that way long ago," Trevor confided. "The senator only came to see you because it had reached the point where if he didn't divorce her, the scandal might break while they were still together and damage his own reputation. Her scandal, I mean."

Loni was developing some kind of feeling for this missing woman. Not respect, exactly, although it did take some nerve to cheat on one's senator husband, if that's what had been happening. It just seemed Joanne Winston had a lot of people arrayed against her and no allies. She must have really missed her murdered friend.

"Did the senator and Mrs. Senator have any kind of financial arrangement as far as you know? Post-nup, anything like that?"

"He gave her a very generous allowance. I wrote that check myself every month when I paid the household bills. As for another source of income, no. Mrs. Winston stopped working at least twenty years ago. She was a mid-level manager for a phone company when they met. Her career path ended at marriage."

Trevor gave her a look to indicate he passed no judgment on such people, but he clearly did. Loni just looked back at him, very professional.

Then, she smiled and extended her hand. "You've been so helpful. Is there anything else you think I should know, knowing my partner and I are representing the senator?"

Trevor looked thoughtful. "If I think of something, I'll let you know. Do you have a card?"

Across the bar, Steve watched Loni scribble her cell phone number on a card and pass it over. Steve shook his head in silent admiration.

Chapter Five

It was Steve's week to use the sailboat. He had been waiting with increasing anticipation for days. He and Loni went down to the marina and boarded the ergonomically designed forty-four foot scow bow. The sailboat timeshare gave Steve and Loni a chance to get on the water in a boat they could not afford on their own, as the upkeep was split three ways as well as the half-a-million-dollar mortgage.

After the purchase, each attorney had dropped a suggestion written on scratch paper in a Baltimore Orioles baseball cap with the agreement that no name of anyone's wife or mother would be used for naming the boat. The Norma Jean, after Marilyn Monroe, was the winner, and she was christened with a bottle of Dom Perignon with all three couples aboard. It was the only time all six of them had been out on the boat together, as the rotation began the next week and no one wanted to share their quiet time with another lawyer. No shop talk; only water, sunshine, occasional romance, and peace.

It was a beautiful day in the Baltimore Harbor where the Patapsco River ended its journey through Maryland. The sky was that blue no painter had ever been able to capture, because no one could recreate the luminosity of the sun behind enough clouds to provide cover but not to obscure the day. They could almost see the crabs dancing below them. Loni didn't love sailing as much as Steve did, but she loved Steve more than he loved sailing, so she went along and acted as crew when Steve needed a deckhand. Besides, evenings on the water could be fun, after the scuppers were keelhauled and the reefs luffed, or whatever the hell one did to shut down a sailboat.

Today, as Steve set the sails and watched the wind indicators on the mast, Loni settled into a chair in the sunshine with a copy of *Against The Law*, a legal thriller she'd recently snagged at a resale bookshop. She was loving the tale of a disbarred lawyer going back into the courtroom.

"How about a beer and a sandwich?" Steve asked after he'd anchored for a lunch break. The beach of a tiny island was in view.

"Sounds yummy," Loni said. "I'll have mine up here on deck." She went on reading. Then, she laughed and they both went down-stairs to the galley. They returned with trays of food and brews in hand to the outdoor dining deck.

"What's your position on Winston?" Loni asked. "Do we roll the dice and take him on?"

"Still undecided. You?" Steve asked.

"Ms. Stands is hiding something, or she may just be loyal to her employers," Loni said.

"Agreed." Steve munched on his sandwich and washed down the bite with a swig of cold beer from a longneck bottle. "That aide, Trevor Prentice, is either more practiced at lying or he's telling the truth and Senator Winston had nothing to do with his wife's disappearance."

"What about the Salinas cold case murder? It doesn't seem to have anything to do with their divorce, or does it?" Loni asked as she wiped her hands on a napkin. Seagulls circled overhead in hopes of a bread crust or potato chip thrown overboard. "A cold case is not something most families have in their backgrounds."

Steve leaned forward on his deck chair. He was wearing a swimsuit and was more tanned than Loni, who was very protective of her skin. It was well worth protecting. She wore a bikini with a T-shirt over the top.

Steve said, "I see that look in your eye. A missing woman, a mystery cold case, and a high-profile divorce all wrapped up in a Washington, D.C. scandal. How can we resist?"

They both knew it was still a crapshoot that they might get caught in the circle of intrigue in a very bad way. It was also possible that they would establish themselves for the final time as the go-to divorce attorneys on the East Coast.

Loni looked at Steve, Steve looked at Loni, and both had a meeting of the minds. The next day, they had Darla deposit the retainer check and Lewis & Lewis became the attorneys of record for Senator James Winston.

But in the meantime . . .

Loni glanced down and said, "I may be getting a little burned."

"Maybe we should go below deck to check on that tender skin."

Loni said, very neutrally, but starting a smile, "You want to go inside?"

He reached over kissed Loni. "No, I meant this below deck," pulling down the waistband of her bikini bottom.

"Hmmm . . . I noticed your interest in my health," she said, tugging down his waistband.

"I'm always like this when you're in sight."

She looked into his eyes, her hand still in place. "I have no way of verifying the accuracy of that."

Steve laughed. "I know, it's the Heisenberg principle. If you're observing . . ."

"Ooh, talk science to me," Loni said. She leaned in for a long, deep kiss. They went below after all.

Chapter Six

The next day, back in his office, Steve looked thoughtfully at the client chair, remembering the man who'd sat there, his attitude that anything could be his for the taking, including any lawyer he wanted. Someday, there might be a point in disabusing him of that. In the meantime, Steve picked up the phone and called the senator to say they'd take on his case and his petition for divorce would be filed the next day.

"Excellent," Winston said over the phone. It sounded like some kind of meeting was going on around him. "But why the delay?"

Because we don't like you much, Steve thought. Into the phone he said, "With a high-profile case like yours, Senator, we need to do some investigating beforehand. Filing the petition will inevitably draw attention. We want to look into the case before reporters swarm all over it."

"Of course," Senator Winston said, properly flattered. Of course, the whole world would be interested in his personal life. "But what is there to investigate?" His voice had shifted from pompous to wary.

"Where your wife is for one thing, but we haven't gotten any-where with that. We've also looked a little into the murder of Sally Salinas."

"Sally?" The background noise diminished as the senator clearly stepped away from the people surrounding him. "This divorce has nothing to do with Sally."

That was interesting. "Would you say your wife's behavior changed before or after Ms. Salinas's death?" Steve asked.

"No." Winston took no time to think about that one. "Sally Salinas had already done her damage to our marriage with whatever she was saying about me."

Another interesting reaction, assuming the best friend had backstabbed him. Steve said nothing, letting the client steer the conversation.

"I assume as the one paying, I get to direct your services," the senator said. Not waiting for an answer, he continued. "So forget about Sally Salinas, file my divorce and get my wife served. I want this over quickly."

"Yes sir," Steve said, and hung up. He stared out his window at the office building across the way.

"What're you staring at?" Loni asked, walking into his office.

"Nothing. Which is exactly what our client wants us to learn about the wife and her murdered best friend."

"Hmm," Loni said.

"Exactly."

She joined him in staring at the fascinating nothing across the way.

Chapter Seven

The senator had been right about generating publicity, of course. Before filing the divorce petition in the local family law court, Steve asked to see Margaret, the clerk in charge of the filing department.

The senator represented a northeastern state but had maintained a second home in a Maryland suburb of D.C. for years, so it was legitimate to claim dual residency and file for the divorce in Maryland.

The family law court clerk's office was a second home to Steve after more than five years of facilitating divorces for his clients. Steve and Loni had established themselves as the best in Baltimore and the place to go if property or children were involved, but they had not stepped up to the level of celebrities or public figures until now. The senator was their first famous client.

Steve waited patiently in line, then moved up to the long counter and asked for a particular clerk by name. In moments, she arrived and with a small gesture brought him behind the counter. The space wasn't private, clerks walked by and a few were at their desks within earshot, but it could be made semi-private with lowered voices. Steve showed her the petition. Margaret raised her eyebrows.

"Yes," he said, looking around, which caused her to do the same. "I'm filing this petition using initials only for the parties. Understand?"

She did. Not her first high-profile divorce filing. Margaret took the pages from him. "Which one of them is famous?"

"Well, semi-famous," Steve said. "Let's just say he holds national office."

"Ah." Again, they were D.C. adjacent, so not the first time around for her. The clerk nodded seriously and knowingly, then glanced at the petition, turning to the grounds for divorce on the second page. "She cheating on him?"

He shrugged. "Depends on whether we need to prove something in court or work out a reasonable settlement. You'll handle it, Margaret? I need my process server to pick it up this afternoon."

"Sure, Steve, don't worry."

Steve thanked her and walked out slowly, pausing to look back. Margaret was taking one clerk aside and getting him started on the filing, whispering to him at length.

They weren't the only interested parties on the other side of the counter. When Steve had said he needed to see Margaret, he'd made sure to say it to the one clerk who was the biggest gossip in the courthouse. After a minute, Steve saw that clerk stroll past Margaret, pausing to listen. The clerk stayed near the petition and even leaned over to question his supervisor. Steve smiled.

Steve went across the street to the criminal courthouse for a minute, stopped in to say hi to a judge, and was in the basement having a cup of coffee when the first reporter caught up to him. Steve glanced at his watch. Eight minutes. Impressive. The one thing that worked efficiently in this building was the gossip line. He suspected it was assisted by regular gifts from a couple of reporters to a few clerks. Clerks were always the ones who knew what was going on in a courthouse.

The reporter recognized him. The most public attention Steve Lewis had ever gotten personally was when he was released from jail and that event drew a lot of coverage, thanks to Loni. He had been held in contempt by a judge who wanted him to reveal something the judge had no right to ask about. The appeals court ordered Steve's release a couple of hours later; he'd spent the interval in pleasant conversation with a couple of deputies inside the jail. He made sure to look a little haggard—but brave, of course—when he walked out, blinking at the sunlight.

"Why's your client filing for divorce?"

"Which client?"

"Ha, ha. Look, you can tell it to me your way or I'll tell it from worse sources. There've been problems in the past."

"His wife left him. It was just one time too many," Steve said.

"Another man?" the reporter asked.

"I have no knowledge. My experience is that when the split comes, there's usually a third party involved. Of course, my experience is as a divorce lawyer."

"Are the police looking into it?"

"We don't know of a crime, adultery no longer being illegal in this state," Steve said.

That made the reporter chuckle. After a little more banter, he left to post his story, first on his blog, then to the online version of the paper. It would be in print by the next day. Another reporter arrived, this one with a camera, but that couldn't do Steve any good. He slipped away, up the stairs, and out to the street.

The senator's comments made the evening news as the networks picked up where the bloggers left off. The senator, of course, handled it well. Expertly. Aggrieved husband still trying to protect his wife's reputation as much as possible.

Ernest Anguish, celebrity anchor on the National News Network, flashed his blue eyes as he did the lead into the story. The crawl along the bottom of the screen read: Exclusive with Senator James Winston.

Ernest looked into the camera. "In a developing story in our nation's capital, it appears that Joanne Winston, wife of Senator James Winston, has gone missing. There are very few details available regarding her disappearance. We go now, live, to Washington where our reporter is speaking with Senator Winston."

The reporter on the street held a microphone to the senator's face.

"I don't know why she left." The senator told all. "I assume she just needed some time alone to sort out her thoughts." That sort of thing.

"Has she done this before?" asked the reporter, leaning into his microphone. "Disappeared without a word to you?"

Senator Winston hesitated. Then, looking even more troubled, he said slowly, "Sometimes she forgets to let me know."

Loni and Steve watched his brief comments on television and glanced at each other with raised eyebrows. The senator was standing on the steps of the Capitol with towering columns as his background.

"Well, that's not contrived," Steve said.

"That little hesitation was brilliant," Loni observed. "Like, he hates to think of how much he's suffered."

Next, Anguish went back to another reporter on the street somewhere around Dupont Circle. The general consensus was that the senator was being truthful. The public seemed charmed by him and gobbled up every word he said. Sound bites from several constituents back in the senator's home district wrapped up the piece.

"Butter would melt in his mouth," Loni said.

"I've never understood that expression. Does that mean he's warm or what?"

"No one understands it," Loni said, standing up. "That's why I like it."

Chapter Eight

L oni spent the evening researching their new client. She went online to GovTrack.us and looked at his voting record. She expected to find a man who'd raped the economy, burned the environment, and attached pork belly legislation to every bill he introduced, but she was surprised.

The senator was fairly moderate in his legislative history. He was a Republican, but not a straight ticket voter. He was not hawkish about the military and had a mixed voting record on the environment. He had been particularly involved in restoring lands to the American Indians and establishing national parks in Wyoming and Utah.

He was quoted as saying, "Give the Indians anything they want."

Was it all for show, or was there a side of the senator that could be trusted after all? She kept delving. Senator Winston was a self-made man who came from humble origins in the Midwest before moving to the East Coast to attend a good college, Dartmouth. Either he was the quintessential American success story, or he'd written his entire Wikipedia page himself. Loni was open to believing anything.

The next morning in their office, Steve glanced at Loni who continued research on her tablet. "I know what you think of him," Steve said.

"No you don't, because I don't know myself. I'm starting to think he's smarter than we gave him credit for being."

"Than you gave him. I never even implied . . ."

"Please." She leaned back in the client chair, stretching her legs. "Wouldn't it be ironic if he was sincere, in real pain right now, but so used to lying and spinning that he sounded fake anyway?"

"You mean like a woman who can't stop herself from making these seductive moves, like body stretching, even when it's no longer remotely necessary?"

"I don't know what you're talking about."

She stood, slowly, and walked around the desk, bending over toward him. Also slowly.

Steve found himself smiling.

"Whatever do you mean?" Loni asked.

Chapter Nine

S teve and Loni waited. They waited to learn the whereabouts of the wife, assuming the senator's people were working on that, so they could have her served, or to get a call from a lawyer representing her saying personal service on her wouldn't be necessary.

That's how it usually worked in a high-profile case. Both sides had resources and could put the case into the hands of lawyers right away. Try to keep it as private as possible. With as much publicity as the case had already received, Mrs. Winston must know about the divorce filing and, if she had any brains at all, she would have already contacted a high-powered divorce lawyer who, in turn, would contact Steve and ask to take the case below the public radar. The other lawyer could also accept service on his client's behalf so she could avoid the unpleasantness of being served. Sometimes high-profile divorces were well on their way to final settlement before the public knew anything about them.

But, a few days went by and the phone didn't ring, at least not with that call.

While they waited, Steve and Loni set appointments up with the Winstons' two grown children. Amelia Scott, thirty-two, now married, and Douglas Winston, twenty-eight, still single, arrived together for the meeting. Darla, paralegal extraordinaire, who'd been read in on the Winston file, ushered the siblings into the conference room and offered them coffee. Amelia, of medium height, blonde by choice, pampered-looking in a designer dress, accepted the offer of coffee, sat immediately, and surveyed the room critically. Her brother, thin with bitten down nails with which he continually scratched his cheek and neck, declined the coffee and paced.

After Darla left them, Steve and Loni listened to them via electronic surveillance in Steve's office.

"I don't know what we can offer," Amelia said. "But thank God they're finally getting divorced. I thought it would end in murder instead."

"Absolutely," Douglas agreed. "They've been angry roommates long enough."

"I thought they were about to work things out until you know what happened," Amelia said. "I wish Mother had never met Sally Salinas. What a troublemaker."

"Always stirring the pot. She definitely made it worse."

"Don't speak ill of the dead, Douglas."

"Oh, only the living? Is that the rule?"

"I don't know if she made it worse. Their marriage might have gone down anyway," Amelia said. "I thought it was nice Mother had a friend."

"I didn't. I almost wish Mother had been there when . . . ." He trailed off.

In the office, Loni and Steve looked at each other. His said *who?* Her shrug answered. They couldn't see the kids'—grown man and woman—expressions, so couldn't quite interpret what they'd just heard. But in response to Steve's shrug toward the door, Loni nodded emphatically.

"We're sorry about your parents' marriage imploding so publicly. From this point on, we want to keep it as quiet as possible. We just wanted to talk to you two to see if you can give us any insight into what the last few years have been like."

That was Loni talking. They had both read the room as soon as they walked in. Douglas leaning against the wall with his arms folded, mad as hell for no reason and undoubtedly not realizing how young he looked. Amelia with an open, bright expression, clearly the smarter of the two. Loni and Steve had decided mutually and without a word that Loni should take the lead now.

"We're sorry about our parents' marriage too," Douglas said.

"Doug," Amelia said sharply. "Have you ever had an unexpressed thought? Try it."

He glared at her, but her gaze held and his didn't. Big sister. Some relationships don't change with time, even if they appear to do so. He put his hands down and abruptly plopped into a chair. It would have made him even madder to know how much he looked like a sullen child.

"So," Loni said. "Maybe we shouldn't have asked you to come. It's an intrusion, absolutely. We know that. But so is a divorce, no matter how old you are. We just wanted to offer you the chance to tell us . . ." She moved her shoulders. "Anything. Or nothing. Whatever you want to say."

Amelia and Douglas, grownups but still their parents' children, exchanged a look and a silent communication, and Amelia turned toward the lawyers. "We'd just like to be left out of it. We don't side with either one, Mother or Dad. Frankly, this day has been a long time coming, and it's about time."

"Do you have any idea of your mother's whereabouts?" Steve asked. "It would speed things up if we could get in touch with her."

"She hasn't texted me," Douglas said, and his sister shook her head.

"I texted her a couple of days ago, something minor, and I haven't heard back from her," Amelia said. "That's not unusual. Sometimes she even loses her phone for two or three days at a time."

Douglas snorted, agreeing. They looked at each other and smiled. This generation couldn't imagine an hour without a phone.

Loni sat between them. "You saw your father's press statement?"

The kids nodded.

"If your mother has gone away with someone, any idea who that might be?" Loni asked.

Douglas leaned toward her, face turning bright red quickly. "You want us to tell you who Mother was most likely to be . . .?" Then, he checked himself, not even having to glance at his sister to rein himself in. "No," he said shortly.

Amelia's silence was much more nuanced. Under Loni's and Steve's combined stares, she shrugged. "A couple of years ago I would have said maybe she'd gone off with her friend Sally Salinas. Just reassessing, you know? I find it really hard to believe Mother's run off with a man. And, it would be totally crazy if Mother was murdered after Sally was murdered."

Her brother shot her a look she didn't return.

Thank God she mentioned this Sally Salinas person in front of us, Steve and Loni thought simultaneously. It would have been awkward telling them they'd been listening in on their earlier conversation. "Who's Sally—what did you say—Salinas?" Steve asked, voice flat as if it was an idle question.

"A friend of Mother's," Amelia said. Her brother interjected, "Only friend." Amelia continued. "Mother met her through . . ." She looked at Douglas, who shrugged. "Just in the neighborhood, I guess. Sally was divorced. I think, just my own personal theory, being friends with her put the idea into Mother's head that there might be life after marriage."

"She was a bad influence," Douglas said, with an expression a parent might use of a child's friend. Loni and Steve exchanged a quick look. It was the same language Barbara Stands had used when they interviewed her at the Winstons' home.

They'd seen this dynamic before in their years of family law practice. Sometimes the children of bad marriages grew up quickly and became protective of one of the bad parents or the other. Or both.

"I thought Ms. Stands told you. She was just a place for Mother to vent," Amelia said. The children looked at each other. After a moment, Douglas started laughing.

"What's funny?" Loni asked.

His laughter winding down, Douglas said, "Just being here. I've pictured this scene for so long."

After a moment, his sister chuckled, too. The hilarity of divorce.

Loni asked, "Sorry to repeat, but any idea where your mother might be right now? This would go much more easily and less publicly if we could talk to her directly. Believe it or not, we want to make this easy on her, too, if we can. Divorce doesn't have to be a war."

Douglas looked lost in thought. "It's not like we had the old family beach house," he said. "Place with fond old family memories she might return to." He looked again to his sister. Amelia clearly had an idea, but shrugged, and said, "It would just be gossip."

"That was the saddest interview I've ever done," Loni said later, stretched out with her legs across Steve's lap back at home. Their abode was a tasteful little place in North Baltimore, the taste supplied by the previous owner who'd done landscaping, put in an interior brick wall, plants in the small yard, all those things neither Loni nor Steve cared to do, but that they appreciated while sitting on the sofa looking around.

"What about that time we got appointed to the guy who killed his girlfriend, her two sisters, and one of their kids and we interviewed her mother?"

Loni looked at him like he was the slow student in the class. "That was sad, sad. She had events inflicted on her. Those kids just sounded like their whole lives were one long slog to this glorious moment with their parents' break-up."

"Sometimes it's like that," Steve said, rubbing her legs. "So I hear. But did we learn anything?"

"Yeah." Loni swirled the ice and amber liquid in her short glass. "Mother had only one friend, who's dead, and the kids don't want us to know something."

"'Only gossip,' Amelia said," Loni mused. "What do you think she meant by that?"

"Babe," Steve said, rubbing her legs a little more deeply, "if we were privy to all the gossip in D.C., we'd own the place."

Chapter Ten

One thing the press does well is dredge up old stories featuring one of the same parties. A couple of days after the senator's divorce filing, Ernest Anguish on his "Ambush News" sequence reworked footage of the senator and Mrs. Winston from a story a year or so earlier that involved them both.

A woman named Sally Salinas had been found murdered in her own kitchen. The story got more attention than it ordinarily would have. First, the murder had gone unsolved. It looked like a case of domestic violence, but the woman was divorced with no known man in her life, so there was no natural suspect. The second reason the story got attention was because the dead woman had been Joanne Winston's best friend. Reporters had tried to work Mrs. Winston into the story as much as possible. All Ernest had at this point, though, was brief footage of the senator's wife giving a sudden loud sob when a reporter had informed her that her friend was dead. Then, she'd slammed the door.

The current story invited speculation. Had Joanne Winston been involved in her friend's murder? Did she know something she hadn't told the police? Had she run away now because she feared arrest? Feared for her own safety? Had she been murdered by the same killer?

Back when the murder story was hot, it was quickly established that the senator had an alibi for the time of the murder, so speculation around him was minimal. No one wanted a defamation of character lawsuit for slandering the senator.

Interest had died down the day after the old story was trotted out, when Mrs. Winston turned up.

But Steve and Loni noticed the rehashed piece. "Sally Salinas?" he asked.

Loni nodded. "That's the one. Douglas thought it was a good thing she was dead. We need to look into her murder."

"Why?" Steve asked, shrugging. "I'm always up for a good unsolved murder, but what's it got to do with our case? I don't think the senator will pay our hours for trying to solve another case, especially one he warned us away from."

Loni turned and looked at him full on. "Then I guess we'll have to hide it, won't we?"

Steve shook his head. "Do not get me in trouble with the State Bar, sweetheart." He reached across and pulled her close. "Or at least make it worth my while."

Chapter Eleven

It didn't happen the way it usually did, but the mystery of Mrs. Winston's whereabouts broke pretty quickly. The senator may have been right about the press being better than the police at that kind of thing, or at least publicity in general. Turn the whole general public into your detective squad and you sometimes get fast results.

Joanne Winston was found literally in bed with another man. The newspaper and television stories had given the public her image and turned a lot of people into amateur sleuths looking under every rock in the Greater Baltimore area, even into neighboring states. Mrs. Winston was reported seen, incorrectly, as far away as Ohio.

A woman who'd rented a room, in the small motel she owned, to a man about midnight a few days earlier began to wonder about the fact she'd never seen his companion, though he obviously had one. He'd been turning away maid service, too, which aroused her suspicions further.

One morning, the man stepped outside, looked around suspiciously for a couple of minutes, then hung a Do Not Disturb sign on his outside doorknob for the fifth day in a row, before going back in. The motel owner decided this was her business after all. Literally.

She gave the man a few minutes to get settled, got a stack of towels and her cell phone, walked across the parking lot, and opened the door with her master key without knocking.

"House . . ." she began, but what she saw made her drop the towels and lift her phone. She snapped half a dozen pictures before the two naked subjects could pull up the sheets and hide their identities, then ran before the man could grab her phone.

The best of the resulting photos showed Joanne Winston's startled face just rising from the pillow, with the sheet pushed down far enough for the viewer to imagine she was naked under the sheet. The man in bed with her was turning away from the camera, which only caught the side of his face, but enough of his bare shoulders, back, and butt to show that he was a man, similarly unclothed.

It was a divorce lawyer's dream. Photographs almost showing the opposing party in the act of adultery. The kind of evidence that usually resulted in a call from another lawyer saying words to the effect of: Just tell me what you want.

The senator called and was almost effusive in his thanks, as if Steve and Loni had set up the photograph themselves.

"I told you filing would do it," he kept saying. Which had actually been his idea, not theirs.

Steve hung up and looked at Loni. NNN was playing on the television that was sitting on the credenza in Steve's office. Ernest Anguish was reporting the story again, with even more enthusiasm as the photo of the two half-naked lovers popped onto the screen.

"Is this really national news?" Loni asked. Steve muted the sound. They didn't look at it again. They were rather sick of it already.

"The client loves us."

"Yay."

"This will probably be our greatest triumph. With huge publicity," Steve said.

"Yay again." Her voice was as flat as her expression.

"And it really stinks, doesn't it?" he asked.

"Like a fish that's been your guest for three days."

She sat on the edge of the desk beside him. "We know anything about the naked guy?" he asked.

She shook her head. Loni hadn't just been reading the papers and watching the news, she'd been making inquiries through her own sources, which were much better. "We think it's someone who'd done a minor sort of job on the senator's last campaign, which was probably how he and Mrs. Winston met. He's dropped out of sight completely now."

"Think he's afraid of the senator's wrath?"

She shrugged. Steve looked at the newspaper photo of Mrs. Winston again. It was grainy, so her expression was hard to read, but her eyes certainly told a story. "She looks awfully surprised, doesn't she?" Loni asked.

"Oh yeah. She wasn't faking that. But the first thing that's so stupid is where she is."

"In bed? Yes. Stupid."

"No," Steve said. "A hundred miles away. Only two or three towns over. If you're going to run away from your famous husband, you need to run farther and faster. And smarter. She had resources. Go to Hawaii or Paris. At least New York, where you could get lost in the crowds."

He'd put his finger on the first thing that had been bothering his partner. Joanne Winston's disappearance had been a national story because of who her husband was, but here, forty minutes from the Capitol where he was a senator, it was inescapable. There could hardly have been a citizen there who hadn't seen a picture of her in the last few days. It was stupid not to get farther before holing up. Steve tried to puzzle it out. "Passion? They just couldn't wait any longer?"

Loni laughed. "That would be your explanation. Spend one night, slake your passion, then put on a hat and big sunglasses and drive like hell out of Dodge. Within the speed limits, of course. Wouldn't want to get stopped by a cop."

He raised an eyebrow at her, laughing. "'Slake your passion'? Is that what you said? Why, Lady Chatterley, how you talk."

Loni joined him in laughing, dropped her shoe to the floor, and pushed on his chest with her foot. "Shut up," she chuckled. "I can use high-falutin' language if I–"

They heard the sound of their front door opening and closing, then a woman's voice calling, "Hello?"

"First of the flood of new business?" Loni made a face.

As they walked down the hall, Steve said, "Maybe she didn't actually have any money yet and they had to wait there until she could get access to it?"

Loni turned the corner, saw their visitor, and stopped. "I don't know," she said. "Why don't we ask her?"

Chapter Twelve

Very shortly into the meeting with their visitor, Joanne Winston, Steve's absence was requested. By his partner. First, they took their visitor into the conference room, where Steve explained to Joanne Winston clearly and at length that he couldn't talk to her if she was represented by a lawyer.

"I'm not," Mrs. Winston said.

"You should be. That's the only legal advice I'm going to give you. Get a lawyer. Anything we do or say will be in your husband's best interests, not yours," Steve said. "He's our client."

"There are no lawyers I trust," she said.

Which begged the question of why she was there. Joanne Winston looked odd in their conference room. She was a few years younger than her husband, very pretty, probably beautiful in the near past and could be again when she chose. Today she didn't. She had a rather long face, with the full mouth and big eyes that photographers love. The cheekbones to go with them, too. But all unadorned this morning. Her eyes looked very tired. She wore slacks, flats, and a simple long-sleeved blouse. Loni thought she had never seen such an expression of disgust coupled with despair. She clearly wanted to take some powerful action, but already knew it would be futile. Her greatest anger was probably with herself.

For doing it, Loni wondered, *or for getting caught?*

Her gaze barely touched them as Mrs. Winston looked out the broad window. "I don't want a lawyer. I know I'm screwed. Just tell me what's the best you can offer me."

"I'll need to consult with my client," Steve said.

"What really happened?" Loni asked.

Steve realized Loni had been looking at Mrs. Winston much more intently than he had. And maybe reading her expression completely differently.

The senator's wife stared back at Loni. Her expression had returned to resigned. "What difference does it make? You've got the pictures . . ."

"What happened to you?" Loni insisted.

Joanne Winston sighed, letting her shoulders ride up and down. "I was drugged and kidnapped. By that man."

Steve almost laughed. "Well, yeah. I guess that's the only way you could possibly . . ."

Loni looked up at him with a hard expression but loving eyes. "Steve, why don't you go make us some coffee or perform some other useless chore that will take you out of this room for a while?"

Loni startled him enough that he stood up without thinking. "No, I . . ." His partner looked at him, he nodded his head slightly and left, closing the door behind him.

In the conference room, Joanne Winston started crying almost at Loni's first words which were, "How did he arrange it?"

"It wasn't subtle. It didn't have to be. I was home one evening while James was working late or at a fundraiser. I didn't bother to keep track of his stories anymore, and that man showed up at my door. I had just gotten ready for bed, but he called through the

50

door that James had left something in his study and needed it right away, so I let him in. He rushed past me so fast I barely got a look at his face. I followed him to the study. I didn't want a stranger rummaging through my house. While I was helping him look for some papers, he put a cloth over my mouth and nose. I struggled. I thought he was killing me. It was very fast-acting."

Loni nodded.

"The next thing I really remember is waking up in that motel with that woman snapping pictures. The man went out the bathroom window, I think. I never did get a good look at him. I just know who he said he was. The police came and somebody called my mother and sister to come get me."

"Did you have yourself tested for drugs?" Loni asked.

"By the time I thought of it probably twenty-four hours had gone past and the doctor said if I'd been put under it was by something that went out of my system quickly. Some can, he said."

Loni nodded.

"I know how stupid my story sounds," Mrs. Winston added. "That's why he arranged it this way, so I'd be left with an unbelievable story. My husband is smart. You have no idea."

"Why?" Loni asked. Joanne Winston lifted her head to stare into Loni's face and Loni just let her, not elaborating on her question.

Apparently, Joanne Winston trusted whatever she saw. She shrugged and said, "James has a tough reelection campaign coming up. He's been cheating on me for years, and if that came out it would ruin him. Leaving me and filing for divorce wouldn't have helped his image either. I think he was afraid of me. He would look at me so strangely sometimes, studying me like he didn't know me.

He'd ask me about Sally, as if I knew something about her death. Lord, I wish I still had her. That's what scared James, I think. That he wasn't sure I'd just go on suffering in silence anymore."

"Why didn't you just leave him?"

"I had the house just the way I wanted it," Joanne Winston said. She put her head back to laugh. Her long, slender neck showed again the beautiful woman she had been. Still was. "I know that sounds silly, but it really is the main reason. Our lives were so separate anyway. He was hardly ever home, we slept separately, we were barely married anyway, without having to go through the mess of divorce. It was my house, I mean I'd made it mine, but James had the money. I didn't want to start over again. I was resigned. And it wasn't a terrible prison. People do worse."

Loni looked thoughtful.

"Tell me about Sally," she said.

Mrs. Winston looked out the window. "She was a good friend. Already divorced when I met her, so she was the cool single friend to the unhappy married woman. As James and I drew apart, Sally and I started spending more time together. She was a realtor, so she often had free time during the day. Our coffee meets turned into happy hours." She hung her head. "Then she was gone."

"Tell me about that," Loni said, settling in.

Steve was watching and listening on the closed circuit TV and thinking about the late best friend, too. He tried to think of a way he could check on Joanne Winston's story, but she hadn't identified the man well enough to check him out. Investigating the rest of her story would involve leaving town. He put in a call to the motel where she'd been found, but the owner/manager was out. He left a message. She was probably getting a lot of calls these days and had stopped answering the phone.

Then, still banned from the conference room, Steve decided to take a drive. He checked the camera first to make sure it was recording everything Loni and Joanne said.

It turned out his car was aimed for the central police station, which surprised him a little. Apparently, there was something useful for him to do. Or maybe it was just curiosity. The average person doesn't have a friend who's the victim of an unsolved murder. It made Joanne Winston unusual in yet another way. Since he couldn't talk to her for the moment, Steve decided to investigate from another angle.

He found himself curious about this Sally Salinas, the best friend Joanne Winston had clearly loved, and the kids, the son, anyway, had disliked in the extreme. A woman who inspired such strong feelings tweaked his interest. Besides, it was the only aspect of the case he could delve into at the moment. The divorce seemed on its way to winding down, now that the opposing party had essentially surrendered. But, Mrs. Winston's surrender itself aroused his sympathy and made him even more curious about her late friend.

At the front desk, Steve asked for a detective he knew. The detective came to the front, greeted Steve, and took him back to the squad room. The bullpen had about six desks, all of them decorated in sloppy housekeeping, with computers several years old. The walls of the hallways had once been white and still were in spots. Steve's detective friend passed him on to the detective handling Sally Salinas's murder.

Tom Sellers had his blue shirt sleeves rolled up, his tie askew, and a three-day growth of beard.

Steve wanted to say, *You working undercover or have you just stopped giving a shit?* But he needed this guy's help. Detective Sellers didn't bother to shake hands. When Steve said the name of the person he was interested in, Sellers sighed as if someone had brought up the girl who broke his heart in high school.

Nodding toward the chair in front of his desk, Sellers said, "That is one cold case, man. Icy. Some idiot is going to get away with that one forever."

"Why do you say idiot?"

Sellers's face started turning red immediately. He stood up and paced around the desk as he talked. "Because it was so damn sloppy. Clues everywhere. It started as strangulation, with Salinas clawing at him, so we've got his DNA from under her fingernails. Probably fingerprints, too, but no one to try to match them to. Neighbors saw a car parked in her driveway, but didn't recognize it, and nobody saw the guy go in or come out. It's just the kind of dumb crime somebody gets away with. If you ever want to get away with murder, don't plan it carefully, don't think, just do it, spur of the moment. Those are the kind of fit-of-passion things that have no closure."

Steve nodded encouragement to continue.

"It was about eight, nine o'clock on a weeknight, can't pin it down any closer than that, everybody was settled in for the night, nobody looking out the window to see the guy come or go, nothing to notice. Nobody found her decaying body till the next day. I can tell you pretty much exactly how it happened, almost anything you'd want to know. I've got the damn case solved. I'm only missing one thing."

"A suspect," Steve said.

"Bingo. Except for her friend, the senator's wife, Sally Salinas seems to have had a pretty empty life. Shitty divorce, evidence of adultery and abuse, but that was three years earlier."

"Did you get DNA samples from the ex?"

Sellers slapped himself on the forehead. "My God, Counselor, that's brilliant. Why didn't I think of that?"

The sarcasm told Steve how much failing to solve the case still stung Detective Sellers.

"Of course we tested the bastard ex-husband. No match. And no one could say they'd seen him there ever. It wasn't the house where they'd lived when they were married. He didn't even have fingerprints in it."

"Hired killer?"

Sellers's tone dropped back into weariness. He shrugged, a full body process, and scratched at his cheek. "The scene didn't look like that. It looked like what I said, sudden passion. She was talking to somebody or arguing with him and then said something that infuriated him. Poor impulse control did the rest. Like I said, it started out as strangulation, then she got loose or he let her go but she clawed at him which enraged him again. Apparently, he caught up the nearest thing, a metal meat tenderizing mallet, and hit her. Hit her just right, in the temple. He ran and she bled out. Very messy scene. We kept all these details quiet, of course. Didn't want to let the killer know how much or how little we had."

"Well, thanks, Detective. Did you . . ." Steve felt ethically shaky even asking the question, but also couldn't help himself. "Did you test Senator Winston?"

"Why would we? It was his wife who was friends with her, not him. He barely had a connection to the dead woman. Oh, I thought about him, sure, when I was getting desperate, but he had an airtight alibi. As I recall, his picture was even in the news and all over social media, attending some event. Fundraiser or something. Not his own event, he was kind of a surprise drop-in, other guests said. But he was definitely there."

Well, good, at least Steve's client wasn't a suspect. His wife wouldn't have that as a bargaining chip in the divorce negotiations.

Detective Sellers's memories showed what a thorough job he'd done, to no avail. Steve thanked him again, avoided answering any questions himself, and left hurriedly. Driving back to the office, he hoped Loni was doing better than he was.

And yes, he thought, *Joanne Winston's story was unbelievable*. Which made Steve inclined to believe her.

In the conference room, Loni asked Joanne Winston, "How did you know the senator was cheating on you?"

"I didn't, definitively. Never caught him at anything. With his schedule, it would have been easy for him. Sally was the one who put me onto it, actually. She knew the signs, from her own

56

divorce. She kept trying to get me to divorce James. My husband overheard her one time and got furious. Called her . . . well, implied that she wanted me for herself. Told me to stop seeing her. When I told Sally that, she got this little smile. Enigmatic."

"Why?"

Mrs. Winston shrugged. "I'm not sure. I didn't ask her."

Loni shot a sharp glance her way. Joanne Winston was looking down at the conference table, at her fingers bunching a tissue Loni had given her. Loni herself felt sure she knew what the late Sally had been thinking. Hostility was sexy. Hot thoughts of one kind turn easily to hot thoughts of another kind. If the senator was the kind of serial adulterer Sally suspected him of being, one of those days he'd hit on her, his wife's best friend. And probably sooner rather than later.

That's what Loni thought. But she surprised her visitor by asking, "Your husband is afraid of you. What do you know that scares him?"

"Me? Scare him? I can't hurt him in any way. He knows that."

"He must think differently or he wouldn't have set this up to make you unbelievable." Surely Joanne Winston had thought of that. She seemed like a bright woman. But now she behaved like a woman coming out of a trance.

Mrs. Winston looked out the window. "James, scared of something I know? I wish I knew what it could be."

Loni continued to watch her, now the side of her face and neck. They were unmarked. Her skin was lovely, in fact. Loni asked the question. "Where was he the night Sally Salinas was murdered?"

"Some event. Two, actually. He apparently left one and went to another. The police never really pinned that down, I don't think. They didn't seem to care about James."

"Were the events close to Sally's house?"

Joanne Winston looked up at her, finally, her eyes wide. "The second one was. Only a few minutes away. Why?"

"What is it you know, Mrs. Winston? Did he say anything when he came in that night? Look different? Anything?"

"Not that I saw. I'd already gone to bed. The next morning, he had a cut on his cheek, but he said he'd done it shaving."

"What is it you know?" Loni repeated. She leaned forward, trying to get the senator's wife to meet her eyes. Usually, Loni's gaze was like a tractor beam, drawing someone in, but it wasn't working with Mrs. Winston. "Something about his habits, his body language, his intentions?"

Mrs. Winston laughed bitterly. "I haven't been able to read him for years." Then, she developed a small crease between her eyes. "I do know one thing. Half the time when people think they know where James is, they're wrong. He has this tricky thing he's done for years. If he's going to a couple of different functions at about the same time, he sends one staffer, usually Trevor Prentice, ahead of him. The staffer goes around telling people, 'Oh yes, the senator and I got here a few minutes ago. He's over there,' meaning across the room or in another room. Sometimes they even pretend to wave to him. Then, when James actually does get there, the staffer would stay on hand for a while, then sneak out and go ahead to the next event and do the same thing. That way people would think James was at each event longer than he actually was. Made them feel they were important to him. And made people think he'd spent a long time at their special event when in fact he was only there for a few minutes. Almost simultaneously somewhere else."

It also meant that people could never quite be sure where he was, Loni thought. *Handy for a man with a penchant for extramarital activities.*

Joanne Winston was looking at her earnestly.

"I have one more question. Who was the man? The one who kidnapped you?"

Joanne's eyes went back down to the tabletop, as if she were embarrassed. She blew her nose in the tissue, tossed it toward the trashcan. "Someone who'd worked for James's campaign. I knew his face, or I wouldn't have let him in. But I never knew his name."

She kept her eyes down.

Chapter Thirteen

The senator's first divorce hearing was on the docket in the Family Law Court of Judge Julia Dougherty for Thursday morning at 10 a.m. This was the senator's home county, some thirty miles from Baltimore, close enough that Steve and/or Loni had appeared here several times. The lawyers met their client outside the courtroom and found a corner where they could whisper without being overheard.

Steve took the lead, because those were the roles they'd established. The senator moved closer to Loni, pretending to be peering over into the courtroom. She subtly slid away. Loni looked at her watch, and Steve thought she was about to remember another appointment or an important phone call.

Pretending obliviousness, Steve said to their client, "As you know, today is all about temporary support for Mrs. Winston. Since she's unemployed and you have control of the funds, the court will make sure she has enough money to live and to hire an attorney while the divorce proceeds."

"What do I have to give up?" Senator Winston asked.

"Nothing right now," Loni said. "Just some temporary support. Enough for her to live on. And somebody will get to stay in the house temporarily. Do you want it?"

Senator Winston shook his head immediately. "It's too much hers. I wouldn't even be comfortable there. Let her stay in the house. I'll be fine. I can sleep in my senate office if nothing else."

That made Loni's eyes narrow. But she said levelly, "That's good. Makes you look like the reasonable one and means less you have to pay her to live on."

Steve added, "And the judge will probably lecture her about getting a job. Does she have a degree?"

Their client nodded. He looked good today. He'd dressed appropriately in a dark suit, as if for the funeral of his marriage.

"Business. MBA, actually. She can get a job. I never said she was dumb. Or inexperienced," the senator said.

Steve went to confer with Mrs. Winston's lawyer, leaving Loni to babysit the client. Loni escorted him into the big courtroom and he stared across at his wife, soon to be ex. Loni tried to read his expression.

Nostalgia? Regret? Sometimes, at this stage, she saw a client look curious, even after a long marriage, wondering what he or she was giving up, what aspect of the spouse the client could have discovered if he'd hung in there. She didn't sense that in James Winston. She felt his anxiety. He just wanted to get away from the woman across the room, which made Loni herself regard the woman curiously.

They wrapped up the temporary orders setting fairly easily. When two people are both ready to end it, there's less niggling about the details, especially since there's nothing permanent about the day's events. Their negotiation was concluded with the parties never coming near enough to touch each other or look into each other's eyes. A handwritten agreement conveyed back and forth across the room commemorated the occasion.

One of the last things the senator said before their signatures were applied to the document was, "I do want to get some things out of the house. Mainly out of my office. And I don't want her to be there when I do it. Now. This afternoon. Preferably right after this."

"She'll want someone to supervise that," Loni said slowly. "Make sure you don't make off with her grandmother's silver, that sort of thing."

The senator shrugged. "Fine. One of the kids. The maid. Hell, her lawyer. Just not her. I don't want to be in the same room with her ever again."

"I think we can arrange that," Steve said. He'd noticed Loni's interest.

So, they got it done, only having to appear before the judge for less than a minute to get her signature on the agreement, turning it into a court order. Loni and Steve shook hands with opposing counsel while their clients sat across the room from each other. When he turned away, Mrs. Winston stared at her husband with a strange expression.

"Okay, what was that look at the senator?" Steve asked when they were in the car headed back to the office.

"I don't know. I really couldn't read his wife." Loni was staring out the window moodily. It really pissed her off when her powers of perception failed her.

"No. Your expression," Steve explained. "You looked at the senator when he said he wanted to get into the house today. What were you thinking?"

"Oh." Her eyes sharpened. "Two things. Earlier, when I asked if he wanted to stay in the house, he said no immediately. No hesitation. He has somewhere else to go. But, and it's a big but, he wants back in right away. He wants to take something away before she has a chance to search the place at her leisure. What might that be?"

They drove on in silence, easily reading each other's thoughts. *Something incriminating?*

Chapter Fourteen

Back at the office, Steve and Loni speculated about the cold case murder of Sally Salinas. It looked like the divorce was going to go through the usual steps, property settlement, sale of any assets to be split between them, then the final decree of divorce. The murder of Joanne Winston's best friend was the only aspect left to stoke their curiosity.

"You aren't going to let this go, are you?" Loni asked.

"Are you?" Steve asked.

"It's like a knock-knock joke without the punch line. I just can't get it off my mind," Loni said.

Steve put it all together. "So, our client doesn't really have an alibi. Sally thought he was going to hit on her at some point, and, that night, between events, he did. In fact, the newspaper said he put in a surprise appearance at the second event, so he rushed over there after he killed Sally?"

"Which was why?" Loni asked. "Why would he kill her?" She turned away from the steering wheel for a moment to look into his eyes. The car never wavered.

For a moment, Steve was distracted, then he shrugged. "She rejected him? The detective said it looked like sudden passion. She made him mad and he flared up quickly. Maybe she said she'd tell his wife? Adultery and divorce, end of his political career. That's why he's afraid of his wife, like you said, if he set her up like that. He's afraid she might figure it out."

"All great," Loni said. "Except we've got the same problem as Detective Sellers. Even if we are right, no proof."

"It's not our job to prove our client is a murderer," Steve said.

"Well, let's say we wanted to find out for ourselves, how would we do that?" Loni asked rhetorically.

"The killer's DNA under the victim's fingernails."

"And how do we get a sample of the senator's?" Steve asked levelly.

"Nearly anything he's touched would have traces of his DNA on it. Get the police to go to his house."

"They don't have enough for a search warrant," Steve said. "If they did, Sellers would have gone there. And, don't forget the tiny detail . . . he's our client."

"We could tell them what we know. None of it comes from the client, we wouldn't be betraying any confidences," Loni said. "It's not about his divorce, only the cold case."

"That's a stretch," Steve said. "I'm as curious about this as you are, but it seems like we're edging close to an ethical line to betray a client, even if it's . . ."

"Don't we have a duty to report evidence of a crime? Never mind, I've got another idea," Loni said.

"I bet you do," Steve said.

"First ask him voluntarily to give the police a sample. Tell him it would help with the divorce if he's been absolutely cleared before Mrs. Winston starts making any crazy accusations," Loni said.

"It might work," Steve said. "If you saw this so quickly, I'm surprised Mrs. Winston hasn't, after thinking about her friend's unsolved murder for three years. If she tells her whole story to her lawyer, who seems pretty sharp, the lawyer will catch on right away."

"Exactly. Pitch it to the senator like that," Loni said.

"You think we ought to alert him that way?" Steve asked.

Loni nodded. "And get him to come in here in person to tell him."

Chapter Fifteen

The meeting with Senator Winston did not go well. The client blustered and threatened and put up obstacles. "Why even let anyone know I was remotely considered a suspect in the Salinas murder? People read something like that and assume you're guilty even if you're cleared and never even arrested. One photo of me coming out of the cop station . . ." He dug his hands into the arms of the client chair as if digging in his heels against his lawyer's suggestion.

"We can arrange it secretly," Steve said, leaning forward from behind his desk.

The senator snorted at the suggestion. "Secretly. Hah. You know who I am. I can't do anything secretly."

Not quite true, Steve thought. *You can be in two places at once.*

Loni leaned toward him, put her hand over his. "This would really help, Senator. It would help the police and that can't be anything but good for your image."

For a moment, he seemed to consider her logic. Then he shook his head adamantly. "Absolutely not. I won't put myself in that position."

After the client stormed out, Loni turned to console Steve. "It doesn't matter," Steve said stonily, looking at the client chair, on which the senator had rubbed his hands so vigorously. "I'll give Detective Sellers a sample of his DNA to test. He must have left plenty on that chair. That's not betraying anything protected by attorney-client privilege, it's just providing evidence of a suspected crime." He looked up at her. "I have to, don't you think so?"

She shrugged. "If you say so. You're the ethics expert. Anyway, I didn't like him from the minute he walked in."

"Doesn't mean he killed her," Steve said. "We have an entire cast of characters to choose from as the murderer."

"Or, a stranger passing through town," Loni said, but didn't mean it.

"Sure," Steve rolled his eyes. "I'm leaning toward Barbara Stands or one of the children. Protect the home at all costs."

"My money's on the senator or Trevor Prentice with Winston's blessing," Loni said. "The senator could have confronted Sally about the trouble she was causing in their marriage and lost his temper."

"I think he's capable of it. I'm not sure I believe he could send his aide over there with instructions to take her out," Steve said.

"Trevor just intuited that's what the senator wanted?" Loni speculated.

"But Detective Sellers said it was an act of passion. A fight that got out of hand," Steve said.

"Maybe, or maybe made to look that way," Loni said.

"Let's say he's right. Maybe one of the children confronted her about the meddling. Children have been known to do that and more to save their parents' marriage," Steve said.

"True," Loni said. "And let's not forget our mystery man who may or may not have kidnapped Joanne Winston. How long has he been around, and would he kill for her if they actually are involved, if her faked kidnapping story is bullshit?"

"Or, kill for the senator if she's right and he set her up?"

Steve found Detective Sellers staking out a cup of coffee in a small diner. He had about the same amount of stubble, even more red-rimmed eyes, and no tie today. He kept his eye on a small house across the street with a newish Ford pickup parked in front of it. Steve made sure not to block his view.

"Any followup on the Sally Salinas case? Any connection with Mrs. Winston's running away or being kidnapped?"

Sellers looked at him out of the corner of one eye. "I interviewed Mrs. Winston. Of course, I followed up on her story; it was the report of a crime. Took fingerprints at the Winstons' home where she said the man had touched things in the process of distracting her. But he's had so many visitors and staff, the findings are worthless."

"Was it maybe Trevor Prentice?"

This time, Sellers turned to give Steve his full attention. "You really have checked up on your client, haven't you?"

A long-suffering looking waitress came by and filled both their coffee cups. Only Steve took the trouble to thank her. Sellers was back to staring at the house and car across the street. "No, Mr. Prentice is not a possible suspect. He's been the senator's aide for years. There's no way Mrs. Winston wouldn't have recognized him, even if she'd only gotten a glimpse."

Sellers stopped. A man had come out of the house across the street, hesitated in the doorway, then sauntered to the truck. He was a vaguely handsome guy, tall, disheveled black hair, shirt not fully buttoned.

No socks, Steve noticed, just black dress shoes. He got in the truck and drove away without looking around.

As the man turned his face toward the diner as he got in his car, Detective Sellers snapped a photo of him with a small camera. The driver didn't appear to notice.

"You need to follow him?"

Sellers shook his head and gave Steve less divided attention. He seemed more relaxed somehow. "You were starting to say?"

"Someone as powerful as the senator always has more than one person working for him. One public aide, like Trevor Prentice, and at least one other the powerful person doesn't like to be seen with in public. The one who never gets invited to dinner with the family. Senator Winston had a guy like that, and it's a strong possibility he's the one who was found in the motel room with Mrs. Winston. I haven't quite got the guy's name yet, but I'm working on it."

"A fixer?" Steve asked.

"Something like that," Sellers said.

Steve was thinking, *If the senator has someone doing his dirty work, how far would that person go to do the senator's bidding?* He looked at the detective and wondered if he should ask that question out loud. But looking at Sellers's bland, knowing expression, he knew the detective had beat him to it by a lot.

"What do you know about the guy?" Steve asked.

Sellers gave him some minimal information, Daniel, no last name, age, height. He'd been occasionally seen by people, including Trevor Prentice, so there were vague descriptions. Steve noted it all and thanked him. The shadow man from Joanne Winston's story was emerging slightly.

Detective Sellers was sipping his coffee in a more relaxed manner. Steve dropped a couple of bills to pay for his own. As he started to scoot out of the booth, he nodded toward the house across the street. "Drug house?"

Sellers shook his head. It didn't appear he'd say anything else, then he suddenly said, "That's my house. And my wife's day off."

Steve said, "Oh," and shrugged in sympathy. Tom Sellers was obviously a good detective. Steve put his card on the table. "If you need a good divorce lawyer, give me a call."

Chapter Sixteen

The sailboat timeshare had cycled back around to Steve and Loni. They decided to spend the night onboard and take advantage of the great weather and a week without any court appearances.

Steve took the helm and Loni untied the last anchor rope, threw it on board, and jumped on as Steve used the small trolling motor to safely release them from the boundaries of the harbor. Loni looked back at the dock and saw a man in a hoodie and sweats watching through binoculars. Something about him seemed familiar and odd.

Is he looking at us or the boat? Or is there someone else out here under surveillance? She looked around the harbor but didn't see anything overtly suspicious. When she looked back at the marina, the guy was gone.

Loni coiled the ropes to prevent tripping and pulled the buoys, that had protected the Norma Jean from the dock, onto the boat. Steve, at the helm, turned the wheel and expertly guided them into open water, cut the motor, and hoisted the mainsail. They were soon speeding along with the wind in their hair and their cares and clients behind in Baltimore.

After tacking several times, Steve took them to port and looked back at land. They could see the skyline of Baltimore in the distance, but no other boats. For their purposes they were alone.

"Want to take a break from all that work and play for a while?" Loni asked with a flirtatious look.

Steve caught her drift and headed upwind. He slacked the sails to a luff so that the boat would drift slowly about. He reached for Loni and began to kiss her gently as he pulled the strings on her bikini top and let it fall to the deck. She kissed him back, took his hand, and led him below and through the galley to the master suite complete with king-sized bed.

They were both undressed and reminding each other of their favorite things when Steve stopped short.

"Do you smell smoke?"

"Yes, I'm on fire," Loni said and pulled him back to her.

"Seriously, I think there's a problem." Steve jumped from the bed and ran into the galley. Loni followed and they both saw a small stream of smoke curling from under the sink and through the air into the vent to the outside.

Steve jerked open the cabinet door and tried to see through the smoke. He didn't want to ignite it further by fanning it. Loni grabbed the fire extinguisher from the wall and pulled the pin. Steve took the red cylinder from her and sprayed inside the cabinet.

Still naked, they both dropped to their knees and looked inside. A small explosive device was duct taped to the drainpipe. It continued to smoke from the area where several wires were inserted into the metal box and attached on the outside to a small cheap-looking timer, counting down the minutes. There were six seconds left.

Steve grabbed Loni's hand and pulled her up the stairs to the upper deck. They ran to starboard and dived over the side into the water as the explosion ripped through the hull of the Norma Jean and took out the entire helm, mainsail, lower and upper decks. Hot shards flew through the air causing Steve and Loni to submerge to avoid the debris. Flames engulfed the floating carcass and, within seconds, the last of the Norma Jean sank below the dark blue water.

Steve and Loni treaded water and looked around for safety. Finding none, Steve, the more experienced swimmer, looked into her eyes.

"Loni, look at me. We can swim. We're safe. Stay calm."

Loni fought her panic as she tread water and judged the distance to shore. "We can't swim that far."

"We're not that far out. We can see land. All we have to do is stay afloat."

"We purposefully chose this spot so no one would come by," Loni said shivering.

Steve pulled her close. "It's going to be okay."

"You're right. You're right." Loni began to get a grip and her mind started problem solving.

"The explosion. Someone would have seen it," she said.

"Exactly. We need to stay close to the explosion. Help is on the way," Steve said, not sure if he believed it. Disbelief turned to relief when he saw a motorboat speeding straight toward them from the land. He let go of Loni and began to jump up out of the water and cross his arms over his head. Loni mimicked him until they were sure that the driver of the boat had seen them.

The Coast Guard crew threw life jackets to them and Loni covered herself as much as she could until the crew lowered a ladder and the two nudes climbed up and fell onto the deck. They were immediately covered with emergency thermal blankets and whisked below where towels, sweatpants, and hoodies were waiting. Steve went back up on deck to see the scattering of debris where his precious boat had been.

Chapter Seventeen

Steve and Loni were deposited back in the Baltimore Harbor on safe ground to a barrage of questions: "What happened? Was it a boat malfunction? What bomb? Why were you naked? Who could have done such a thing?"

The two answered all of the investigators' questions, finally convincing the Coast Guard officials that they were not drug traffickers or some other type of criminal. They were asked if they wanted to call an attorney and both laughed.

"No, but we'd like to call Detective Sellers at BPD," Steve said.

Detective Sellers met with Steve and Loni in the Coast Guard office with his own set of questions. After an initial understanding of the facts surrounding the explosion, he asked, "Any clients unhappy about their bill?"

"We handle divorces. Everyone's unhappy about everything when they come to us," Loni said.

"Both sides," Steve said.

"Any threats lately?" Sellers asked.

"No, but . . ." Loni said.

"No, but what?" Sellers asked.

"I saw a guy in a black jacket on shore watching us with binoculars when we motored out. Something about him seemed odd."

"You didn't mention anything to me," Steve said.

"Just a feeling at the time, but now it seems obvious it was more," Loni said.

"Any idea who might have taken it to this level?" Sellers asked.

Steve and Loni looked at each other.

"We've been looking into the Salinas murder. Just asking around, but it sure seems like a coincidence," Steve said.

"Jesus! I told you to stay away from that. Can you give me a description of the guy you saw?"

Loni shook her head mournfully. "Only what I just did. Black jacket, binoculars. Kind of a big guy. White." She shrugged.

Steve was thinking, *Maybe the guy you told me about, the one who does the senator's less public bidding?* If Sellers didn't reach that conclusion on his own, Steve would suggest it privately.

When he and Loni were alone for a few minutes, he told her about the fixer.

She looked thoughtful, barefoot in her borrowed clothes. "I wonder if Mrs. Winston ever met this mystery man," she said.

Steve's jaw was clenched and he was glaring at nothing. "I don't know, but someone tried to kill us. This makes up my mind on the ethics question."

"What ethics question?" Sellers asked.

Steve just shook his head.

Sellers had BPD specialists canvas the Lewis's home and office for additional bombs, but they found nothing. The courthouse had sniffer dogs and metal detectors already installed, so they assumed the couple would be safe when there.

After a quick visit to his own office, Steve followed the detective back to police headquarters and into the squad room. Sellers looked up in surprise since they had just parted a few minutes earlier.

"I hope I'm about to make your day," Steve said. "Maybe your career." Steve held up a large plastic bag holding two long swatches of dark fabric.

"You kill something and skin it?" Sellers asked.

"Yes. My client chair. Specifically, its arms, covered in someone's DNA. Someone who might be a suspect in the Salinas murder."

Sellers's eyes widened. The men talked a few minutes longer, and Steve left the evidence in Detective Sellers's grateful hands.

The next day, in their office, Steve and Loni met with Sellers yet again.

"After I saw you in your office, your guards freaked out when they heard about it. They only want us to go home, here, and court. They say we're safest in those three buildings." He and Loni had asked Sellers to come by to discuss the pending investigation.

"I would tend to agree with them," Sellers said.

"Anything new on the closed circuit cameras at the marina?" Steve asked.

"Yeah, we have a picture of the bastard who climbed on your boat with a duffel bag, presumably holding the bomb, but his face is obscured. What we can see is blurred. I'm having it enhanced, but no guarantees."

"Too bad," Steve said.

"Obviously, we have no fingerprints since the boat is at the bottom of the sea, but a couple of promising tattoos peeking out of his sleeve could help," Sellers said. "And you?"

"Well, we were thinking," Loni said. "If we're going to soak up all your manpower and be under a microscope, we might as well make it count for something."

"Right," Steve joined in. "Why not let your guys go dark? Make it look like you've watched us long enough, then use us for bait. We need to meet with the Winston family and the senator's aide, Trevor Prentice. Those are our main suspects."

"Maybe we can flush this guy out into the open and go back to our lives," Loni said. "If he doesn't come back, we haven't lost anything."

"You two are crazier than you look," Sellers said.

Chapter Eighteen

In their office, with the arrival of Mrs. Winston and her lawyer imminent, Steve said, "Listen, in this negotiation, why don't you play the good cop for a change and I'll be the growling asshole."

Loni put a hand over his. She was wearing black skinny leg pants and a white blouse that made her skin glow. That skin in turn made her green eyes pop. "Much as I'd love to see that performance, love of my life, I have something else to do."

"You're not going to be here for the settlement conference?" Steve's slump made his disappointment obvious.

She cocked her head with a smile. "I think you can handle it, sweetheart. Her, with her ridiculous story, caught in bed with another man on the front pages of several area newspapers? You can reel that one in yourself."

"Yeah, but it's fun to play back and . . . never mind. What are you going to do, make some calls?"

She stood up and slung her purse over her shoulder. "No, I'm actually going out into people world."

Steve's brows drew together and a little V formed above his nose. "The police specifically asked us not to go out. Or have you already arranged for undercover backup?"

"No." She smiled down at him. "I've arranged to have a life. When I want to put cops in charge of my life, I'll let them know. Don't worry." She set down her purse and briefly pulled out something to show him. She reached across the table and stroked his cheek, then walked out.

She'll be fine. Steve wasn't worried. He frowned at the closing door and resisted the urge to call Detective Sellers or advise their security detail.

Loni was walking toward her car in the garage when a hand grabbed her arm and pulled her roughly to the side. She gave a little shriek, but the garage was empty except for her and her assailant. Detective Sellers had apparently granted their request to have their protection detail back off.

At the moment, Loni wished they were still hovering.

The assailant let go of her arm.

Loni whirled, ready to strike. Then she stopped, staring at the grim face of Joanne Winston. Loni looked quickly down at the woman''s hands and saw they were empty.

What's going on?

Now she saw Joanne Winston looked frightened, not angry. Her hand when she pulled it away from Loni's arm trembled. Her face was very pale. She drew them aside into a shadowed corner.

"Are you all right?" their client's wife asked. "I heard what happened to you on the boat. I'm so sorry. That must have been terrifying."

Loni nodded slowly, puzzled. "It was, thank you. But I can't talk to you, Mrs. Winston. You're represented by counsel now and we're on the opposite side."

Joanne shook her head. "We're not on the opposite side of attempted murder. That's all I want to talk to you about. I'm on my way into your office for the negotiation, yes, but I was hoping to take you aside at some point anyway. I feel awful for you."

"Thank you." Loni had relaxed. She let her senses roam around the garage and still felt no one else there. She wasn't being set up. At least she didn't think so. "Thanks for your sympathy, but I really have to . . ."

Joanne Winston shook her head. "I'm worried about you. But don't you see? I'm terrified for myself."

Now Loni saw that was true. When she and Steve had first seen their client's wife she'd looked worn out, resigned to her fate. Now, her eyes were red, both hands shook, and she kept darting sweeping gazes around the dim garage.

"What is it?" Loni asked.

"I think I might be next," the senator's wife said. "If someone tried to kill you, why not me? It would be James, of course. And there's something else. Remember at the end of our negotiation in the courthouse, the temporary orders hearing? James said he wanted to come back into the house without me there. Did he tell you why?"

Loni shook her head slowly.

The door to the building opened and out walked a member of the security detail wearing plainclothes. Joanne Winston jumped. He looked at Loni who gave him an "all is okay" nod.

"Do you know why he wanted back in the house?" Loni asked to refocus the conversation.

85

"I don't know why either," Joanne said. "I can't figure it out. I've looked all over for something missing and I can't find anything. My attorney accompanied James, but he said he didn't stick with him too closely. The only places he went were his office and my bedroom."

"Do you use the office too?"

Joanne shook her head. "No. He used to be strictly private about it, but he probably figured I'd sort it out after he left. I've looked through it, but if there's something missing I wouldn't know. He always kept the place such a mess."

"Ours was a bomb," Loni said. "Have you had your place swept for anything like that?"

She shook her head again. "I wouldn't have any idea how to go about that."

"Maybe you should check into a hotel for a few days," Loni said, drawing away. "Or stay with your daughter. I'm sorry, that's all I can suggest. I really have to go, Mrs. Winston. I feel like I've broken some rule already."

She was turning to leave when Joanne Winston said, "That's not it." Loni turned back to her, cocking her head to show she was paying attention. "I'm not worried he took something," Mrs. Winston continued. "I'm worried he planted something. Not a bomb, some . . . something. Some piece of false evidence tying me to something."

"That's a little farfetched, Mrs. Winston. If you want to hire a private detective, just ask your lawyer for a suggestion."

"I just wanted you to know." Loni was walking quickly away now, but the other woman's words came to her clearly, echoing in the garage. "If something happens to me, just remember. Please."

"Thanks for coming," Steve said. He was in his own conference room, with Mrs. Winston and her lawyer, Roger Cunningham, one of the better and more congenial family lawyers in the area. But he wasn't known for his cutthroat courtroom skills. Joanne Winston had obviously given up any idea of going to court. It was just a question of what kind of settlement she could get.

Steve was at the head of the table. Senator Winston sat to his right, his chair half turned away, like a sulking child at a dinner featuring spinach. His wife was watching him steadily. He wouldn't return the gaze.

Roger's younger associate, whom he'd introduced as Robin Young, sat to Steve's left with Roger beside her and Mrs. Winston a couple of chairs further down.

"Can I get anyone coffee? Iced tea? Soft drink? Those little tea cakes with icing? Cucumber sandwiches?" Steve asked.

Roger laughed.

Ms. Young, unsmiling, said, "I've been told about your sense of humor. No thank you to any of that." She snapped open her briefcase, lifted its lid, beautiful brown leather, looking both soft and tough, and pulled out a short stack of papers. "Here's our proposal. The summary is on the first two pages, the rest are supporting documents. One copy for you and one for your client."

She handed them over and Steve passed one to Senator Winston. Steve had barely glanced at it when there was a snort of outrage from his right. The senator whirled and glared at his wife. "More than half? You want fifty-five percent of our assets after you've proven yourself the slut of the western world? How you have the nerve . . ."

He slammed his fist down on the sturdy mahogany table. Must have hurt, but he didn't flinch.

His wife looked back at him blandly. "There's that on the one hand . . ." She actually held out a hand. "Versus thirty-five years of cheating and being an asshole on the other."

The senator's head grew so bright red instantly Steve felt he should open a valve to release the pressure. He stood, took his client aside, whispered in his ear, and guided him to the door. "Excuse us," he said to the room over his shoulder.

He led his client down the hall, Winston ranting and fuming. The word bitch got overused to the point it lost all meaning, with others taking its place in spots.

Steve steered him into his office and closed the door. "Some negotiations go better if the client is removed from the immediate process. This appears to be one of those occasions."

"I should just go home now," Winston fumed, beginning to pace. "This is clearly a waste of time. I've got an important vote this afternoon."

Yes, we all know how important you are, Steve thought.

"You can leave whenever you want, Senator. We're not going to reach any final agreement today and, of course, we won't reach any agreement at all without your approval and signature."

The client exhaled and visibly calmed down, but only slightly. "You've got a new client chair," he said in an odd voice. He touched the object in question, a more high-tech affair than the previous one, chrome and vinyl.

"Just trying it out," Steve said. "Feel free to sit at my desk if you want. Use the computer, the phone. Darla will get you whatever you need." He walked to the door and turned. "By the way, Senator, that was a good opening outrage. I liked it, it played well for us." He smiled and went out, closing the door behind him.

Striding back to the conference room, he thought, *Bullshit. You have a temper, Mr. Senator. And it flares suddenly.*

"Well, sorry about that." Steve took his seat in the conference room and smiled at everyone. "Where were we? Oh yes." He looked down at the opening proposal, then took the top two pages, tore them neatly down the middle, then across, dropped them in the small recycling bin, smiled at opposing counsel, and said, "Bold opening proposal, Roger. It's much to your credit. But it's also what my client said." He turned to the younger lawyer. "Did he say nonsense or bullshit?"

Young didn't smile back, just looked at him. Turned to her senior employer. He nodded. Young took another set of clipped pages out of her briefcase. "Proposal two," she announced, and passed it over.

Steve looked down the table at Mrs. Winston. She looked nice today, in a pale green blouse. She looked like she'd been to a spa since they'd last met, or at least gotten a massage. Her skin was firm, and she was expertly made up. She looked back at him and shrugged. Steve did the same with his head.

Chapter Nineteen

L oni walked along a street in Georgetown, not feeling observed except in the usual way, by men passing by. She didn't
sense hostility from them, though. She turned a corner, abruptly
did an about-face and came back around the same corner. She saw
nothing amiss, no one ducking into a doorway, no obvious undercover cop trying to look like a druggie trying to score. God knows
no homeless people. Georgetown cops scooped them up and took
them briskly across the state line into Maryland.

She found the brownstone she was looking for, one of those
great old homes with a stoop where a family could live. She
walked up to the front door and buzzed one of the buttons.

After a rather long delay a youngish man's voice said, "Yes?"

In response, Loni said her name. There was a pause she took
to be surprise on the other end. It was just about to reach the breaking point where she was leaning forward to say, "I'm here to . . ."
when the door buzzed and she went in.

God, she loved these old Georgetown mansions that had been
broken up into apartments or condos. Hardwood floors, beautiful thick walls, a staircase that must once have seen Jackie Ken-
nedy descending. Loni went up, appreciating the polished wooden
handrail, and proceeded along the hall. She knocked at 2C, the last

one on the right. Again, she felt a long hesitation on the other side, then the door opened quickly, framing a surprised-looking Trevor Prentice.

When an invitation wasn't immediately forthcoming, Loni stepped across the threshold saying, "May I?"

"Of course," Prentice said, waving her toward the spacious living room. "To what do I owe the pleasure?" It seemed a sign of his discomfiture that he fell into cliché.

"Just want to clear up a couple of questions I have."

"You could have called."

She could have, but then she couldn't have watched his face and body language when she asked her questions.

In the high-ceilinged, airy living room Douglas Winston sat on the white sofa. Loni had a sixth sense for reading people and situations and, from the exaggerated ease of Douglas's posture—legs crossed, arm extended along the back of the sofa—she felt quite sure he'd considered hiding in the bedroom until she was gone rather than being here to greet her.

"Welcome," he said, then stood to shake her hand. He flopped back down onto the sofa with boyish loose-jointedness, nothing like his famous father.

Loni looked back and forth between them. "Did you think I might be coming?"

Doug looked baffled. "No. Just visiting."

"Douglas and I happen to be friends," Trevor said, waving her down to the sofa and taking a seat himself in a wing-backed armchair.

"Ah."

The syllable somehow seemed to make the senator's son defensive. "Why not?" he said. "Trevor's spent so much time at the house helping Dad, I saw him more than I did Dad. Or Mother." Douglas suddenly reached out and touched Loni's knee. "By the way, thank you for whatever your part was in getting her back home. Amelia and I were so worried . . ."

"I'm glad." Loni said nothing about the huge tension that must have accompanied his mother's homecoming, given the circumstances. "I'm glad she turned up safely."

Douglas seemed more introspective than she'd seen him before. "I was more worried than I probably let on, but it's been a huge relief to have her home in one piece. Once you know someone who's been murdered," he said, looking down at the floor, "you realize it's a possibility, that anyone's story can end that way. I didn't like Ms. Salinas, but I felt terrible for her, dying that way."

"I got that impression before," Loni said. "Your dislike of Sally. Why? Did she treat you badly?"

"Oh, no. She was fine with Amelia and me. I just thought she pulled my mother away from the family. And she was a bad influence. Mother would say they were going to happy hour, then she'd come home drunk at ten o'clock at night and head straight for her bedroom."

"Plus . . ." Trevor said mildly.

Doug glanced at him, then at Loni. "I believe Mother's explanation for what happened. But if she ever did . . . have an affair, it would have been because her friend Sally led her down that path."

"What?" No one had ever suggested anything like this. But Loni hadn't forgotten Mrs. Winston's mention of her friend's knowing little smile when she told Sally about her husband's rant against her.

"Oh, yes," Trevor said. He'd obviously wanted his friend to broach this subject, but then he jumped into it. "That woman was shameless. Everyone knew what a—well . . ." He suddenly grew a little prim. Then said, "She even hit on me once. Quite obviously."

"What?" Doug stared at him.

"Yes." The smug look appeared natural on Trevor's face. "What's so strange about that? She'd had at least one too many at a little party at your parents' house and cornered me. It would have been flattering if I hadn't been nearly overcome by the fumes."

"You didn't?" Doug asked. He was leaning forward, elbows on knees, to look at his friend.

Trevor made a face back at him. "God, no. I have my standards. Besides, it would have been . . . Well, she was swaying a little bit while she was leaning into me. It would have been . . ."

"Un-chivalrous?" Loni suggested. She was leaning back, soaking in the information. And the exchanges between the two young men.

Trevor chuckled. "Yes, I guess that's the old-fashioned term for it."

Doug looked at her rather shyly, then his eyes widened and he reached a hand toward her. "Oh, God, I hadn't even thought about it until right now. We heard about what happened with you and your partner. Your boat blown up right underneath you! Are you all right?" His sympathy sounded genuine.

"Yes. But still in danger according to the police, because they haven't found the bomber."

"Horrible," Trevor added. "If we can do anything."

"Thank you. I appreciate it. The police have security footage of the guy who planted the bomb, but it's so grainy you really can't even tell—" A thought stopped her briefly, then she shook her head. To Douglas she said, "You mentioned something the other day at our office. 'Just gossip,' you said. I hate to pry, but given everything that's happened, even gossip might lead somewhere. Did this gossip you mentioned have to do with Sally Salinas and . . ." She found it hard to say the words. ". . . your dad, maybe?"

The young man's eyes widened and he put up his hands. "Dad? Oh, God no. He hated that woman. No one would ever have thought that. No, the gossip was about . . ." He looked at Trevor.

Trevor took mercy on him. "There's always gossip about people in positions of power. And this is D.C. The four estates: legislative, executive, judicial, and gossip. That's all some people have to do. But I think the particular gossip to which Douglas was referring was about the senator and his housekeeper."

"Mrs. Stands?" Loni was genuinely shocked. *The stately, rather severe British servant?*

"Ms. Stands," Trevor corrected her. "Never married, never attached to anyone as far as anyone knew. I don't think there was a word of truth to that gossip, and I quashed it whenever I heard it. But people will talk. She's worked for the senator for a long time and is fiercely loyal to him."

Douglas chuckled. "Don't get between Dad and Ms. Stands if she thinks someone is being rude to him. They'll be out the door so fast you'll see 'whoosh' marks in the air."

This is getting me nowhere, Loni thought. She didn't even consider it worthwhile gossip. The senator and the housekeeper, in the throes of passion? God, there was an image she was never going to be able to erase.

"One other thing," she said, hastily changing topics. "We heard something about someone else who works for the senator. Someone who might get asked to do things that aren't so much in your line, Trevor."

He looked puzzled. "What do you mean? My line is everything."

"The senator might use this other person for assignments that are more . . ." She was trying to avoid using a word like criminal or illegal because she was pretty sure that would get her nowhere. Trevor was too loyal. "More physical, you might say."

Trevor still looked blank. But from her side Douglas said, "You must mean Brad."

She turned to him. "Do I?"

"He came to the house sometimes. He was an ex-cop, looked like he could really handle himself. I think Dad stopped using him, though. Brad was a little scary. I don't think Dad thought he could rein him in anymore. But he used to come around fairly often. Even sometimes when Dad wasn't in. He'd arrive early and wait for Dad to come home."

"Brad. Do you know his last name?"

"Holman, I think?" Douglas looked at Trevor, but Trevor still wasn't saying anything. "Oh my God, I just remembered something. I think when Brad was a cop he was on the bomb squad. Something got him fired, though."

"Bomb squad?" Loni asked.

"He could be mad at Dad for firing him. Is it possible Brad could have thought Dad was on the boat with you, or supposed to be, or something?"

Loni sat stunned. No, she didn't see how someone could have thought that. But if he'd planted the bomb sometime before Loni and Steve arrived, not knowing who might be with them, he might get lucky. With pieces of Steve and Loni floating on the water as collateral damage.

Chapter Twenty

B y the time she got to her next stop, Loni had calmed herself down. Anyone who would plant a bomb was a coward, wanting no confrontation with his victims.

He wouldn't pull a drive-by shooting on a busy street in the daytime would he? Loni kept looking over her shoulder and both ways down side streets just in case.

Detective Sellers looked less run down this morning. Maybe that's because it was Loni standing across the desk from him.

"So how can I help you, Miss? We don't have anything new on the sailboat bomber."

"Start with not calling me Miss." She smiled to take the sting out of it and neither of them looked offended. "I came by because I have some new potential information on the bombing you might want to look into." She told him about Brad Holman, who used to do mysterious errands for the senator and had a history with bombs. She left it to the detective to determine if Holman had been working for or against Winston when he'd planted this particular bomb.

"Hmm," Sellers said, looking thoughtful.

"I also wanted to talk to you about the Sally Salinas murder," Loni said.

Sellers got that girl-who-broke-my-heart-in-high-school look again. "Ow. This was starting out to be a good day. Haven't you learned your lesson about meddling?"

"It could still be a good day. I came to ask about the DNA evidence Steve brought you. The fabric swatches from the client chair."

"Still no result. I'll let you know."

"Well, I heard you have the new black box in the station here," Loni said.

"How'd you know about that?"

"A criminal lawyer friend of Steve's said the BPD used it as evidence in a bail hearing against one of her clients."

"Right, bail hearing. Not trial. It's still experimental and we don't know how useful it will be," Sellers said. "It's being used around the country as a threshold evidentiary tool, but the courts haven't yet shown their confidence in it."

"How about you? Do you have confidence in it?" Loni asked.

"About ninety-eight percent. Every time I've used it as a screening tool, the lab DNA tests verified the initial findings."

"That's enough for me," Loni said.

"And might this suspect have a name? That might speed up my detecting."

"Yes. Like all of us, this suspect has a name. I'll tell it to you when you tell me whether this sample matches the DNA found under Sally Salinas's fingernails. Deal?"

Sellers stood up and pointed a finger at her. "Look, Miss . . ." He stopped. "Ma'am wouldn't be any better than Miss, would it?" he asked.

Loni shook her head slowly, making the detective feel he was at least teachable. "Then what?"

"How about Loni?" She extended her hand and he shook it, feeling strangely privileged.

"Look, Loni, if you have evidence of a crime, you have an obligation to give it to me."

"We won't know if it's evidence of a crime until you test it, will we?"

She smiled. He didn't, not at first, then he shook his head, with a "you got me" look.

"Now," Loni said. "Tell me about this Sally Salinas. For some reason, I feel like I know her, but you actually investigated her." She leaned across the desk and batted her eyes at him. "And I'm sure you're a wonderful detective."

They both laughed at her Marilyn Monroe impression. Loni had found that some men needed to be flattered. Others, better ones, liked seeing just a glimpse of her real self, the no-BS good lawyer. She was starting to like Tom Sellers.

"Sally Salinas," he said reminiscently, as if he'd known her too. "Interesting woman. I am genuinely sorry her life got cut short. I would have liked to have known her. Except she scared me a little bit, too. People said she had an almost hypnotic effect on people. Very charming."

Loni leaned forward with sparkling eyes and listened to more tales of Sally The Seductress. By the time Sellers finished, Loni was developing a theory. More than one, actually. Before she left, she said, "By the way, did you meet the senator's housekeeper in the course of your investigation? Ms. Stands?"

"I tried, but she wasn't available. She was in England at the time of the Salinas murder. She has a sister who was very sick, and she was there over a month taking care of her. She'd been gone for a while when Sally Salinas was killed and wasn't back until weeks later. Why?" Detective Sellers looked ready to write something down.

"No reason," Loni said, her disappointment evident.

Chapter Twenty-One

Steve met with the senator after their negotiation with Mrs. Winston and her attorneys ended. After its rocky start, things had gone more smoothly, Mrs. Winston acknowledging again her position was difficult. Steve thought he saw an end in sight to the divorce side of the case.

"Excellent," the senator said. "If she'll just acknowledge what she did was wrong, I might be inclined to be more generous."

"She is the mother of your children, after all."

"She is that." The senator had mellowed considerably this afternoon.

The door flung open and back against the wall. The senator almost jumped out of the client chair.

Steve did jump. "What the hell?"

"Sorry. Miscalculated." Loni strolled in, staring at the client, and not in a comforting way.

"The negotiation went well," Steve said, hoping to restore the atmosphere to what it had been before the entrance of his partner.

"Great," she said flatly. To the senator she said, "When's the last time you talked to Brad Holman?"

His eyes widened a little, but he tried to appear unperturbed. "Where did you hear about Brad?"

"The point is I did hear about him, and what I heard wasn't good. I don't want something about him to jump up and bite us before we get your divorce finalized."

The senator shrugged. "Nothing to worry about there. I haven't talked to Brad in months. I hear he's gone into private practice as a detective."

"Great," she said, flatly again. Steve was looking back and forth between the two.

Suddenly Loni smiled. "Everything's fine then!"

"What? Our own client?" Steve asked.

Said client was gone now, and Loni had told Steve what she'd learned. Their boat had been bombed. Their client sometimes employed a man who had worked with bombs. It was too huge a coincidence.

"But why?"

"Maybe we were asking too many questions about Sally Salinas, he thought we were getting too close," Loni said.

Steve stood up and paced with her. They were both too rattled to sit.

"Douglas Winston shared the information," Loni said. "But Doug is too loyal to his father to think he might be the one behind having us killed."

Steve gave that another few seconds' thought, then obviously switched back to the senator. "Whether Doug is right or not, we can't accuse him without evidence."

"Nope," Loni said.

The next time they passed, Steve said. "But if the DNA samples come back matching, we've got motive for Winston to sic his hired killer on us."

"Absolutely," Loni said.

"I'm going to call Sellers and ask if they've got the results yet," Steve said.

"They don't. I just came from there. Maybe tomorrow. Oh, and he shot down another theory of mine without knowing it." She explained, concluding, "If the senator and Ms. Stands were really a secret item, and she thought he was being lured away by Sally, she might have gone there for a confrontation. Or maybe if she was just so loyal to her employer and thought Sally was bad news."

"You suspected Ms. Stands? Of killing Sally Salinas? That's a hell of a stretch."

"She could have done it. She wouldn't have to be all that strong. The killer didn't strangle Sally. She was hit on the head with a meat hammer. A woman could do that."

"I guess."

They looked at each other. It was going to be a long night waiting for the DNA results tomorrow.

They Ubered home, neither of them wanting to turn their key in the car ignition.

Back at home, Loni told Steve about her unexpected meeting with Mrs. Winston in the parking garage. "She seemed genuinely scared."

"I did wonder why Winston wanted to go back in the house himself, when he could have just asked the housekeeper to bring him whatever he wanted," Steve mused, trying to picture the senator rummaging hastily through his own home.

"His wife speculated he was leaving something, not taking something. Planting evidence to incriminate her," Loni added. She flung herself down on the sofa, stretched out her legs, and kicked off her shoes.

"What could he possibly have planted? The police have the murder weapon. Any blood he might have taken away from the scene would have been on his own clothes. That's not going to hurt his wife."

Steve joined her on the sofa and in thinking. "Maybe a note?" Loni asked. "Something in writing from Sally Salinas?"

"Don't you think something like that would have turned up by now? This is too weird. She must have been hallucinating."

"I'm telling you, though." Loni repeated, "She was genuinely scared."

"Tell her to go to the police."

"I did. Is there anything else we can do?"

Steve snapped his fingers and pointed at her. "I know. Let's meet with our client and tell him not to kill his wife."

Loni rolled her eyes. "Brilliant, Holmes."

Then they both went silent.

Chapter Twenty-Two

Steve practically camped out in Detective Sellers's office the next day, with a team of undercover officers watching Loni back at the other office. Steve had been managing to discuss baseball and other manly distractions when Sellers's phone finally rang.

"Detective Sellers." He put his hand over the receiver and mouthed *"Lab."*

"Uh-huh. You're sure? Get someone else to check it, too, will you, Lucy? I want to be damn sure about this one."

He hung up. He had an expression like the girl who broke his heart in high school had sent him a Christmas card with a picture of her and her lovely family. "Nothing," he said. "No match."

"You're kidding. You're sure?"

"Lucy is the DNA chemist, and I've never known her to be wrong. She says there's not even close to a match with what she found under Sally Salinas's fingernails and the DNA on what you brought me."

Steve stood up slowly. Sellers looked even more disappointed than Steve felt, and he didn't even know the stakes.

As he walked out, Sellers called, "Whose DNA was that, by the way?"

Steve just shook his head and kept walking.

Back in their building, Steve walked into Loni's office and low-ered himself into her own client chair. His face was carefully neutral. "Want to know the DNA results?"

Loni lounged at her desk, her long legs stretched out. "I'm pretty sure I do know."

"But you said you suspected our client from the beginning."

"I didn't say I suspected him, I said I didn't like him. There's a difference."

"The senator didn't do it," Steve said.

"Thought so," Loni said.

"Then who?"

"I'm working on a theory. Let's go for a drive."

Chapter Twenty-Three

They easily eluded the cops who were supposed to be guarding them. This was a Loni and Steve investigation now, not to be shared with anyone else at this near-final stage. Besides, they had always taken care of each other.

"I found pictures of Brad Holman online," Loni said as she drove, the breeze from her open window making her hair ripple. "There is almost nothing until recently when he apparently did become a private investigator. Now, he posts for publicity."

She handed Steve a photo of a man in a suit, looking right into the camera, square jaw, forthright chin. Everything about him was like that: squared off. Even his eyes, which gave off an *I'm more of a man than you are, pal* self-confidence.

"What does a woman see in that face?" he asked.

Loni glanced at it. "This woman sees a smug asshole. Here's one I even found on Facebook with him at the beach, plunging into the waves." Sure enough, there was the same square guy, this time with broad bare shoulders, looking back over one of them grinning as the foam soared up around him.

"That must bring in the business."

Loni was thinking of Brad Holman, and not in a good way, as she drove through the streets of the small town of Farmingville. Formerly a farming community, it was now apparently dependent on the highway to stay alive: fast food places, slightly nicer restaurants, bungalows, and finally the motel into whose courtyard Loni drove.

With all the other choices, it was hard to imagine why anyone would choose this one to spend the night, certainly not several nights. Courtyard Inn wasn't exactly shabby, but it was . . . well, no, it was shabby. Peeling white paint, scraggly grass completely failing to cover the dirt of the square in the middle that gave it its name.

This was where Joanne Winston had been caught in bed with a man not her husband. Luckily, the owner/manager was in, a woman with her hair up and a white blouse over too-tight gray pants. The office was tiny, cooled only by a small window-unit air conditioner that somehow made it warmer inside than outside.

When she discovered they weren't going to rent a room, Mrs. Warner was less than thrilled with them, but she did agree to look through the handful of photos. She looked at the full-face shot, said, "I didn't get a view of him like this, but it looks like him." She stopped at the beach shot. "Oh yeah, that's him," she said almost immediately.

"How can you tell?" Steve asked. It wasn't a very good shot of Brad Holman. One could see a little of his face, but mainly he was turned away. Loni pointedly didn't ask anything.

Mrs. Warner started out a little demure, which did not fit her age or dress or anything about her, then she lifted a hand. "That's the view I had of him when he turned to get out of bed and away.

Those shoulders. That's him, all right." She looked up and saw the two lawyers looking at her, evaluating her credibility. "I remember his shoulders," she said defensively. "Sue me."

"So, it was the senator's fixer who kidnapped his wife," Steve said on the drive back. "How does that help us?"

"Former fixer."

"Yes, if you believe him."

"We no longer have a motive for why our client would want to have his wife kidnapped. Or us killed. Not since we know definitively he didn't kill Sally Salinas."

They drove in silence.

Chapter Twenty-Four

Steve and Loni sat at their law firm in Loni's office. Steve stretched out on the loveseat with a pillow propping up his back and shoulders.

"I've developed my theory," Loni said. "Want to hear it?"

Steve sank further into the short sofa. "You mean changed it completely, like you sometimes do in mid-trial? Sure, go ahead."

"Yes, I'm flexible. Thank you." Loni grew animated behind her desk, leaning over it. "Sally Salinas understood that you could not like a man but still want to seduce him. It's a power thing, for a certain kind of woman. You told me there were accusations of adultery in her divorce, but I looked into that. All the accusations were against her. Seemed to be something to it, too, since she agreed to a settlement that was very good for her husband."

"You think she was having an affair with the senator?"

"Not necessarily an affair. Maybe a short flirtation or one-time fling. Something she could secretly hold over his head. And Mrs. Winston knew it."

"What?" Steve looked surprised.

"Or at least suspected. Our client's wife said she told her best friend her husband thought she was a bitch and her best friend just smiled. A woman in that moment doesn't see a little secretive smile flit across her best friend's face and not ask her what she's thinking. Especially when the subject under discussion is the first woman's husband. She'd ask unless she thought she knew. If Joanne Winston had said she asked but Sally wouldn't say, I might have believed that. But I call BS on her version."

"That's kind of a stretch."

Loni shrugged, that shrug that moved more than just her shoulders. "I already knew she was a liar, so I was working from that. Add it to the background on Sally and it adds up."

"Me too," Steve said. "But I couldn't see how it fit."

Loni raised an eyebrow to ask the question, and he continued. "She said she let that supposed kidnapper into her house late at night when she was ready for bed, but she didn't even get his name or know enough about him for the police to track him down. Crap. She knew him. She was having an affair with him. Went off on some week-long love fest, as the senator said she'd done before. Probably hadn't even heard any news, so she didn't know there was a big hunt on for her. That's why they didn't bother to run farther than they did," Steve said.

"Exactly," Loni said, joining him. "Plus, she said the police came and her mother and sister took her home, but she didn't tell them the kidnapping story and none of them suggested taking her to a doctor?" She shook her head. "Her mother and sister would know her well enough to get the story from her or see signs she was drugged. No. They didn't take her for drug testing because she hadn't told them that version of the facts. She didn't tell that story because she hadn't thought of it yet."

"So, she came to us to do damage control," Steve said.

"More than that. To put suspicion on her husband of killing her best friend. She probably figured there might be evidence that they'd been together. At least it might have come out that no one could actually testify definitely that he was somewhere else at the time of the murder. She didn't know the police had DNA from Sally Salinas, because they hadn't released that information."

"Create a bigger problem for him to distract him from suspicion of her for adultery. And once people started thinking of the senator as a criminal type, it would make her story that he'd had her kidnapped more believable."

Loni nodded. Steve moved to the client chair and looked closely at her. "So, she just told you the story of her friend's little secret smile and expected you to put it all together from that?"

"We'd been talking for a while by then, but more, it was intuition. A feeling." Loni grew her own secret smile.

"Well, interesting story," Steve said. "Let's get this divorce done and be free of these crazy people."

"Oh, I think we'll wrap that up pretty quickly. Once Joanne Winston is arrested for murder."

Steve had been just getting up, but now he sank back in the client chair. "What?" he asked.

"You said Detective Sellers was very thorough. Got DNA samples from every possible suspect. But, he made one stupid assumption, that the killer was a man. Why? Because it took a man to strangle her?"

Steve had gotten over his surprise. "Right. The killer didn't strangle her. The detective said it started out as strangulation, but that just means somebody grabbed Sally around the throat. A woman could do that."

"Yes. A furious woman who'd just found out her husband was cheating on her with her supposed best friend. Then, Mrs. Winston let her go but Sally scratched her and made her mad all over again. So, Mrs. Winston grabbed a kitchen implement and hit her."

"A man would have just punched her," Steve said.

Loni nodded. "Exactly. Once I thought of the idea that maybe Ms. Stands killed Sally, I realized it could have been a woman. Any woman. And, after the struggle, the killer panicked and fled. Again, as easily a woman as a man. A case could be made that it was manslaughter, not murder, or even just negligent homicide. That's probably how Mrs. Winston will try to spin it once she knows they've got her dead to rights."

Steve was staring at her. She raised her eyebrows.

He said, "And I suppose you can prove all this?"

"The police can, once they have her DNA to test." Loni pulled a plastic bag from her pocket. Inside was a tissue, the one Joanne Winston had used to blow her nose. Loni dropped it on her desk, and they both studied it for a minute, until Steve carefully picked it up and put it back in the bag.

Chapter Twenty-Five

"I would never do this under normal circumstances," Detective Sellers said. "Civilians at an arrest? Never." He looked at them grudgingly. "But you two earned it."

"Why, Detective, that is so sweet," Loni said. He turned to her as if being genuinely complimented, then realized she was messing with him. They laughed. Steve didn't join in.

"What about the guy who tried to kill us?" he asked, dead serious.

"My team made some really tedious comparisons to the lousy photos of the guy we had who looks like the one who planted the device."

"Bomb," Steve and Loni said together. Device was so impersonal. Bomb was devastating.

"Whatever. Looks like the same guy who worked for the senator and was found in his wife's bed at Courtyard Inn. Plus, he wasn't as careful as he thought. He left some DNA on the sheets at the motel and some more on the dock where your boat was docked."

Sellers turned to Steve. "Remember what I told you about stupid guys getting away with crimes? I love chasing the smart ones. They get too cute for their own good."

Steve shrugged. The wait was stretching out. "Anyway, Mrs. Winston killed her best friend, that's pretty definitive, then tried to bury her guilt at sea with you two. Her boyfriend had the bomb squad experience. At least, I'm pretty sure he was her boyfriend."

"Oh yeah," Loni said. "After young Douglas told me the man came to their house at times when the senator wasn't even there, that was pretty easy to figure out, assuming Joanne Winston was really having an affair, which I think we've established now."

"Like everyone says her friend Sally was trying to lead her to do," Steve said. "Besides, it also means . . ."

Loni took it up. "If he'd spent that much time with the family, Mrs. Winston certainly would have recognized him the night he showed up to 'kidnap' her. Since she said she didn't really recognize the guy, it was just too obvious that she was lying."

"Yeah, but kill for her?" Sellers asked.

"Must have been really good between them," Steve said. "I've heard of these rare cases where a man would do. . . " His partner elbowed him in the ribs and they both burst out laughing.

Sellers rolled his eyes. He tensed. "Here they come."

It turned out it had taken three uniformed officers to pull Mrs. Winston out of the family manse without looking like they were roughing her up. She was screaming, cursing, trying to kick them.

"Assholes! How much is he paying you? Do your damn jobs. Help! Storm troopers. My husband is . . ."

She looked over and saw the little trio at the edge of the arrest scene in front of her lovely home that she had gotten just the way she liked it. Her eyes went fierce and narrow. There was very little trace of the elegant, beautiful woman Loni had originally met in their office.

"Bastards! You were working for him all along," the senator's wife said.

Steve said quietly but in a voice that carried, "I told you that the first time we met."

Joanne Winston started screaming again. "Sally and I were lovers! That's right. It got a little rough sometimes. I wasn't there that night, but that's why my DNA was under her fingernails! It was probably always there."

She started cursing again, and the officers pulled her as gently as possible to the patrol car and drove stately away, no siren needed.

The other three gave each other looks featuring raised eyebrows.

"Uh," Steve said.

"Gotta admire her for coming up with a defense that fast," Loni shot back.

"Except for one thing," Detective Sellers said. "No one told her there was DNA under Sally Salinas's fingernails. Outside you, me, and the ME, there's only one person who would know that."

On the drive home, Steve said, "But you said Joanne Winston seemed genuinely scared when she accosted you in the garage."

"I've figured that out too."

"Of course you have."

"Of course I have. She was scared. Of getting caught for killing her friend. She was desperately trying to throw suspicion back on her husband."

119

Steve made a little sound of agreement. "Plus, once she'd told you he might have planted some fake incriminating evidence in their house, if something like that did turn up she would have already explained it away."

Loni nodded. "And all it cost her was a little acting in a dimly lit garage."

"If that's all she had in mind," Steve said. "We don't know what might have happened if Security hadn't checked on you."

Loni shivered. "Either way, she got what she wanted. Harm me or cast suspicion."

Which she probably enjoyed, Loni thought.

Chapter Twenty-Six

Their client took them to a beautiful dinner and gave them an even more beautiful check. The restaurant was one of those heavily paneled places that dated back almost to the Mayflower.

People Loni and Steve vaguely recognized as Very Important People kept dropping by to say hello to the senator. Loni thought one fellow senator might even kiss his ring, but, at the last minute, he controlled himself.

Loni had lobster, while Steve enjoyed a bloody ribeye steak. A hearty cabernet sauvignon rounded out the meal. Winston fully enjoyed himself in the wine department, so two bottles were required. Both Steve and Loni thought the food and wine made the company a lot more bearable.

The Winston children were not invited, and Steve and Loni had not been told whether they sided with Mother or Dad. Probably fell back into the loving arms of Ms. Stands.

Senator Winston introduced all the movers and shakers to Steve and Loni, his so-called brilliant lawyers. They got it: if they were brilliant they must have been hired by someone even smarter. So, they remained unimpressed, and got away before the brandy, looking back to see the senator being joined by others, a couple of them young and very pretty.

"Told you I didn't like him from the beginning," Loni said.

"He's exactly the guy that walked into the office on the first day," Steve said.

A few days later, Detective Sellers called and added a little more detail, just for the two of them. Steve was recapping the conversation for Loni. They were sitting on the same side of a booth in their favorite restaurant, which specialized in Maryland crab cakes and strong drinks.

They'd looked at several used sailboats earlier that day, thinking they might buy their own with the fee from the senator. Plus, with the new business coming in, it seemed they'd be able to afford it. Those VIPs that had not impressed them had very impressive checkbooks.

"Sellers said Senator Winston didn't seem surprised when he found out it was her," Steve said.

"That was the look he gave her in court. He knew she was the killer. He wanted as far from her as possible," Loni said.

"Joanne Winston realized there was only one good way to go and blamed everything on her partner, Brad Holman. Admitted she ran off with him."

"Because that's no crime," they said together.

Steve nodded and continued. "But then said it was totally his idea to plant the bomb in our boat because we were so mean to her, accusing her of stuff." He rolled his eyes. "Detective Sellers played it beautifully. Once he relayed that to Brad, Brad started giving them all the evidence on her. I think they finally accused each other of plotting Pearl Harbor."

"True love," Loni sang, then added, "What did Joanne Winston say when she was interviewed?"

Steve chewed his crab cake and gave her an *Um, this is scrumptious* look.

Two could play at that game. Loni looked back at him with a slow smile, meaning *You could spend the night in this restaurant. Or the car.*

Steve took her hand. "This is the best part. Mrs. Winston said, 'It was her, wasn't it? That woman at the lawyer's office.'"

"She knew I figured it out?" Loni asked.

Steve looked her in the eyes. "He said she didn't seem the least bit surprised."

THE END

BULLET BOOKS
SPEED READS ➤

ON A PLANE . . . ON A TRAIN . . . FASTER THAN A SPEEDING BULLET!

BULLET BOOKS are speed reads for the busy traveler, commuter, or beach-goer. All are new original crime fiction stories that can be read in two to three hours. Gripping cinematic mysteries and thrillers by your favorite authors!

Page turners for fans who want to escape into a good read.

ALL ABOARD!

www.bulletbooksspeedreads.com

Leave a Review

If you enjoyed this book, please leave a REVIEW on Amazon or Goodreads. Reviews are the lifeblood of authors and often determine whether other readers purchase books when they shop. Thank you.

Keep up with the latest books and giveaways here:

www.bulletbooksspeedreads.com
www.starpathbooks.com
www.facebook.com/bulletbooksspeedreads/

Jay Brandon

Jay Brandon is the author of 19 novels which have been published around the world, including *Against the Law*, which *Booklist* called, "a fine tense legal thriller with an offbeat plot." *Shadows Knight's Mate* has been called "an absorbing, exciting, and absolutely entertaining novel." Jay's legal thriller, *Running with the Dead,* was called by Kirkus "a brilliant entry in a series that just keeps getting better." His earlier novels include *Fade the Heat*, was an Edgar finalist. A short story, "A Jury of his Peers," which was chosen for *The Best American Mystery Stories of the Year*, by Otto Penzler and Lee Child. His Bullet Book, *Man in the Client Chair* debuted in Fall 2019. Jay has a master's degree in writing from Johns Hopkins University.

www.jaybrandon.com

Manning Wolfe

Manning Wolfe, an award-winning author and attorney residing in Austin, Texas, writes cinematic-style, fast-paced crime fiction. Her legal thriller series features Austin Lawyer Merit Bridges. Manning is co-author of the popular Bullet Books Speed Reads, a series of crime fiction books for readers on the go.

As a graduate of Rice University and the University of Texas School of Law, Manning's experience has given her a voyeur's peek into some shady characters' lives and a front row seat to watch the good people who stand against them.

www.manningwolfe.com

This book is a work of fiction. Names, characters, places, and incidents either are products of the author's imagination or are used fictitiously. Any resemblance to actual events or locales or persons, living or dead, is entirely coincidental.

Starpath Books, LLC
Austin, Texas
www.starpathbooks.com

Bullet Books Speed Reads and Starpath Books, LLC provide authors for speaking events such as book clubs, book signings and library presentations. To find out more, go to www.starpathbooks.com or email: media@ starpathbooks.com.

ISBN EBook: 978-1-944225-26-1
ISBN Paperback: 978-1-944225-27-8

10 9 8 7 6 5 4 3 2 1

Printed in the United States of America

Made in the
USA
Lexington, KY